BOUND TO HER
DESERT CAPTOR

BOUND TO HER DESERT CAPTOR

MICHELLE CONDER

MILLS & BOON

First published in Great Britain 2018
by Mills & Boon, an imprint of HarperCollins*Publishers*
1 London Bridge Street, London, SE1 9GF

Large Print edition 2018

© 2018 Michelle Conder

ISBN: 978-0-263-07436-9

MIX
Paper from
responsible sources
FSC
www.fsc.org **FSC C007454**

This book is produced from independently certified
FSC™ paper to ensure responsible forest management.
For more information visit www.harpercollins.co.uk/green.

Printed and bound in Great Britain
by CPI Group (UK) Ltd, Croydon, CR0 4YY

This is for Robyn,
who is always warm and welcoming
no matter what.
Thanks for taking care of my dad.

CHAPTER ONE

'I'M SORRY, YOUR MAJESTY, but there has been no further information as to your sister's whereabouts.'

Jaeger al-Hadrid, King of Santara, nodded once then turned his back on his silver-haired senior aide. He stared out of the arched windows of his palace office on to the city of Aran below. It was early, the dawn sun bouncing off the Gulf of Ma'an and bathing the sleepy capital of Santara in a golden glow. The pale pink palace perched on the crest of a hill faced the once industrious port that had recently been transformed into a tourist mecca: hotels, restaurants and shopping outlets, tastefully designed to blend the old with the new. It was just one of Jaeger's successful attention-grabbing visions to boost the local economy and showcase the changing face of his kingdom.

He didn't see any of it right now, his mind locked down by the worry brought about by his sister's disappearance.

Where was she? And, more importantly, was she all right?

A week ago he had returned from a business trip to London to find a note on his desk.

Dear Jag,
I know you won't like this but I've taken off for a few weeks. I'm not going to tell you where I'm going because this is important to me. That's why I haven't taken my cell phone.
No doubt if I did you'd figure out where I'm going before I even get there! But don't worry, I'll be fine.
I love you,
Milena xxx

Don't worry? Don't worry? After what had happened three years ago, how could he do anything but worry?

He reached for the note on his desk, now enclosed in an evidence bag, and had to force himself not to crumple it in his fist. So far the only thing his elite security team had been able to find out was that she had taken a flight to Athens and then disappeared with a man. A man who had been identified as Chad James. An employee, no less, whom Jaeger had personally allowed his sister to work alongside for the past six months.

His jaw hardened and he had to force himself to breathe deeply. Chad James was a brilliant graduate who had been recruited from the States last year to work for his pet company, GeoTech Industries. The company only employed high-energy, intelligent men and women who could think outside the box to create leading-edge technologies that rivalled anything coming out of Silicon Valley. A week ago the young graduate had put in for one month's leave without pay.

Had he coerced Milena into going with him for some lovers' tryst? Or, worse, kidnapped her and planted the note, planning to ask for a ransom any day now?

Jag cursed silently. Since becoming King a decade ago he'd done his best to keep his siblings safe from harm. How had he failed so extraordinarily in that endeavour? How had he got it so spectacularly wrong? Again! Because it *was* his fault. He'd put his sister in harm's way, even if he hadn't known it at the time, and he held himself *fully responsible*.

And it couldn't have come at a worse time.

For the past decade he had worked tirelessly

to pull Santara out of the economic and political quagmire his father had inadvertently left it in, and, right when he was on the verge of having Santara recognised as an integral political power-house on the world stage, his sister went missing.

The worry was eating him alive.

'How is it possible,' he growled in Tarik's direction, 'that in this day and age no one can find out where she is?'

The elderly man Jag had known since his boy-hood shook his head. 'Without her mobile phone or computer there's no way to track her,' Tarik answered, not telling him anything he didn't already know. 'We have accessed security footage in and around the ports of Piraeus, Rafina and Lavrio, as well as the local train stations, but so far we have come up empty-handed.'

A knock at the door cut off Jag's vicious string of curse words. His PA entered, and murmured something to Tarik before casting him a quick, sympathetic glance.

Jaeger's heart thumped into his throat. Please don't let his sister be in trouble.

Noticing his granite-like expression, Tarik shook his head. *No, not the Princess.*

Jag let out a rough breath. Only his tight inner

circle knew that Milena was missing. Together they had mobilised a small taskforce of elite soldiers to hunt for her and Chad James, demanding absolute silence in the meantime. Jag hadn't even alerted his brother to Milena's disappearance and he didn't plan to until he had something concrete to give him. Nor had he alerted the Crown Prince of Toran whom Milena was due to marry in a month's time.

The last thing he needed was a scandal of this magnitude, a week out from hosting one of the most important international summits in Santara's history. Leaders from all over the globe would be descending on Santara for four days to discuss world matters including environmental affairs, world health issues, banking and trade deficits. It would be the largest summit of its kind; a pinnacle moment in Santara's rebirth, and his staff had worked tirelessly to see that it came off without a hitch.

'Tell me,' he demanded, noticing the slight hesitation on his aide's pale face.

'I have just been informed that Chad James's older sister landed in Santara an hour ago.'

Jag frowned. 'The sister he emailed the day before he disappeared?'

'I believe so. A report on her has been sent to your inbox.'

Jag sat down at his desk, touching the mouse pad on his computer to awaken the screen. Quickly he found the relevant email, scanned it, and opened the attachment. It was a dossier of sorts.

Name: Regan James
Age: Twenty-five

Height, weight and social security number were all there. Her eyes were brown, her hair brown, and she worked at some posh-sounding school as a teacher. According to the report, she lived alone in Brooklyn, and volunteered at a bereavement centre for kids. No pets and no known convictions or outstanding warrants for her arrest. Parents deceased.

Which Jag already knew from the file that had been compiled on her brother. She also had a photography website. Jaeger flicked to the next page. On it was a photo of Regan James. It was a half-body shot of her standing on a beach somewhere, her hair tied back in a low ponytail, wisps of it caught by the breeze on the day and flattering her oval-shaped face, her hand raised as if to keep it back. She was smiling, a full-faced smile, showing even white teeth. A camera hung around her slender neck, resting between her breasts. It was a photo of a beautiful woman who didn't look as if she would hurt a fly. And her hair wasn't brown. Not in this photo. It was more auburn. Or russet. And her eyes weren't just brown either, they were…they were… Jag frowned, caught his train of thought and shut it down. They were brown, just as the report said.

'Where is she now?'

'She booked into the Santara International. That's all we know.'

Jag stared at the photo that shimmered on his screen. This woman's brother had taken his sister somewhere and he would move heaven and earth to find them and bring Milena home.

He only hoped Chad James had an army to help him when he finally got his hands around the bastard's scrawny neck, because nothing else would be able to.

'Have her followed,' Jag ordered. 'I want to know where she goes, who she talks to, what she eats and how often she goes to the bathroom. If the woman so much as buys a packet of gum I want to know about it. Is that clear?'

'Crystal, Your Majesty.'

Regan knew as soon as she walked into the shisha bar that she should turn right back around and walk out again. All day she'd trudged around the city of Aran looking for information on Chad, but the only thing she'd learned was that there was hot and then there was *desert* hot.

Despite that, she knew that she would have fallen in love with the ancient walled city if she were here for any other reason than to find out what had happened to her brother. Unfortunately the more she had searched the city for him the more worried she had become. Which was why she couldn't follow her instinct now and leave the small, dimly lit bar Chad had frequented, no matter how tempting that might be.

The dinky little bar was dressed with various-sized wooden tables and chairs that looked to be filled with mostly local men playing cards or smoking a hookah. Sometimes both. Lilting Arabic music played from some unknown source and the air seemed to be perfumed with a fruity scent she couldn't place. Not wanting to be caught staring, she straightened the scarf she had draped over her head and shoulders in deference to the local custom, and wound her way to the scarred wooden bar lined with faded red leather stools.

The truth was this place was almost her last resort. All day she'd been stymied either by her own sense of inadequacy in trying to navigate the confusing streets of Aran, or by the local people she met who were nowhere near as approachable as the travel-friendly propaganda would suggest. Especially Chad's weasel-like landlord, who had flicked her with a dismissive gaze and informed her that he would not open the apartment without permission from the tenant himself. Having just come from GlobalTech Industries, where she couldn't get anyone at all to answer her questions, Regan hadn't been in the mood to be told no. She'd threatened to sue the shifty little man and when he'd responded by informing her that he would call the police she had said not to bother—she'd go there herself.

Unfortunately the officer on duty had told her that Chad hadn't been missing long enough to warrant an investigation and that she should come back the next day. Everything in Santara functioned at a much slower pace than she was used to. She remembered it was one of the things Chad enjoyed most about the country, but when you were desperate it was hard to appreciate.

Utterly spent and weighed down by both jet lag and worry, she'd nearly cried all over the unhelpful officer. Then she'd remembered Chad mentioning this shisha bar so after a quick shower she had asked for directions from one of the hotel staff. Usually when she went out in New York it was with Penny, and right now she wished she'd persuaded Penny to come with her because she didn't feel completely comfortable arriving at an unknown bar alone. She felt as though everyone was watching her and, truth be told, she'd felt like that all day.

Most likely she was being overly dramatic because she was weighed down by a deep-seated sense of dread that something awful had happened to her brother. She'd felt it as soon as she'd received his off-the-cuff email a week ago warning her not to try and contact him over the next little while because he would be unreachable.

For a man who was so attached to his phone that she often joked it was his 'best friend', that was enough to raise a number of red flags in her head and, try as she might, she hadn't been able to dispel them. A spill-over effect, no doubt, from when she'd had to take over parenting him when he was fourteen. Still, she might have been able to set her worry aside if it hadn't been for her friend and work colleague, Penny, who had regaled her with every morbid story she could remember about how travellers and foreign workers went missing in faraway lands, never to be heard from again.

For two days Regan had ignored her growing fear and tried to contact Chad, but when she'd continued to have no luck Penny had almost bought her the plane ticket to Santara herself. 'Go and make sure everything is okay,' Penny had insisted. 'You won't be any good to the kids here until you do. Plus, you've never been on a decent holiday in the whole time I've known you. At best you'll have a great adventure, at worst...' She'd left the statement unfinished other than to say 'And for God's sake be careful,' which hadn't exactly filled Regan with a lot of confidence.

As she cast a quick glance around the bar as if she knew exactly what she was doing, her gaze was momentarily snagged by a shadowy figure in the far right corner. He was dressed all in black with a *keffiyeh* or *shemagh* of some sort on his head, his wide-shouldered frame relaxed and un-moving in a rickety wooden chair, his long legs extending out from beneath the table. She wasn't sure what it was about him that gave her pause but nor could she shake the feeling that he was dangerous.

A shiver raced down her spine and she told herself not to be paranoid. Still, she felt for the can of mace in her handbag and, satisfied that it was there, pinned a smile on her face and turned towards the bar. A man as big as a fridge stood behind the counter, drying a glass, his expression one of utter boredom.

'What'll it be?' he asked, his voice as rough as chipped cement. As far as greetings went it fell far short of the welcome mark.

'I don't need anything,' Regan began politely. 'I'm looking for a man.'

The bartender's brow rose slowly over black beetled eyes. 'Many men here.'

'Oh, no.' Regan fumbled in her pocket when she realised how that had sounded and pulled out a recent photo of Chad. 'I'm looking for this man.'

The bartender eyed the photo. 'Never seen him before.'

'Are you sure?' She frowned. 'I know he comes here. He said so.'

'I'm sure,' he said, clearly unamused at being questioned. He reached for another glass and started drying it with a dishtowel that looked as if it hadn't seen the inside of a washing machine for days. Maybe weeks. 'You want hookah? I have strawberry, blackberry and peach.' Which would explain the fruity scent she'd noticed when she'd first walked in.

'No, I don't want a hookah,' she said with a note of defeat in her voice. What she needed, she realised, was some sort of guide. Someone who could help her navigate the streets and widen her search for Chad.

She'd thought about hiring a car while she was here but the Santarians drove on the opposite side of the road to what she was used to and, anyway, Regan's sense of direction was not one of her strong points. Some might even call it one of her worst. At least Chad would. Remembering how he had often teased her about how he could turn her in a circle and she wouldn't know which way was north made a lump form in her throat. The thought of never seeing her brother again was too much to bear. He'd been her lifeline after their parents had died. The one thing that had kept her total despair at losing them at bay.

'Suit yourself,' the human fridge grumbled, ambling back down the bar to a waiting customer in local dress. In fact, most of the patrons were dressed in various forms of Arabic clothing. Everyone except the man in the corner. She cast a covetous glance in his direction to find that he was still watching her. And he hadn't moved a muscle. Was he even breathing?

Determined to ignore him, she strengthened her resolve and shoved a dizzying sense of tiredness aside. She was here to find Chad and no oversized bartender, or man in black, was going to put her off. Feeling better, she clutched Chad's photo tightly in her hand and started to move from table to table, asking if anyone knew him or had seen him recently. Of course, no one knew anything, but then, what had she expected? It was just a continuation of the theme of the day. As she grew more and more despondent it wasn't until she had stopped at a large table of men playing baccarat that she realised that the low-level conversation in the bar had dwindled to almost nothing.

Suddenly nervous, she smiled at the men and

asked if any of them knew Chad. A couple of them smiled back, their eyes wandering over her. Regan felt the need to cover herself with her hands but knew that she looked perfectly respectable in cotton trousers and a white blouse, the scarf covering her unruly brown hair. One of the men leaned back in his chair, his tone suggestive as he made a comment in Santarian. The other men at the table laughed and Regan knew that whatever he'd said, it hadn't been pleasant. She might be on the other side of the world but some things were universal.

'Okay, thanks for your help,' she said, giving them all her stern schoolteacher look before turning her back and quickly moving to the next table.

Which, unfortunately, was *his* table.

Her gaze skimmed across the table with the untouched hookah on it to his hands folded across his lean abdomen. From there it travelled up the buttons of his shirtfront to his tanned neck and square jaw. Moistening her lips with the tip of her tongue, Regan vaguely registered a sensual unsmiling mouth, a hawk-like nose and the most piercing sapphire-blue eyes she had ever seen. And that was as far as she got. As if she was caught in the crosshairs of a predator's glare she stood frozen to the spot, her gaze held prisoner by his. His eyes glittered with a lethal energy that was startling and Regan had the sudden realisation that she'd never come across a more dangerous-looking or unapproachable man in her life. Her heart palpitated wildly inside her chest as if she'd just stepped in quicksand and was about to sink.

Run! echoed throughout her head but, try as she might, she couldn't make her body obey. Because not only was he dangerous-looking, but he was also sinfully good-looking, and, just as that thought hit, so did a wave of unbridled heat that raced through her whole body and warmed her face.

Good lord, what was she doing noticing his looks at a time like this?

She blinked, her sluggish brain struggling to register her options. Before she could come up with something plausible he moved, kicking the chair opposite him away from the table and blocking her avenue of escape. The sound of the chair scraping across the stone floor made her jump, and once more her heart took off at a gallop.

'Sit down.' His lips twisted into a mocking smile. 'If you know what's good for you.'

His voice was deep and powerful, commanding her to obey even though she knew it was stupid to do so.

This close she could see that he was far more physically imposing than she'd first thought, and completely, unashamedly male. He looked strong enough to be able to pick her up one-handed and take her wherever he pleased. With a start she realised she might not be completely against the idea. A ripple of excitement coursed through her, making her feel even more light-headed than the jet lag.

This was insane.

This *thinking* was insane. She did not react to men like this. Especially not men who looked as if they meandered on the wrong side of the law and won. Every time. Still, what could possibly happen to her in a bar full of patrons? Patrons who were still watching her with curious eyes.

Driven by the need to get out from under those curious glances, she chased off the inner voice of doubt and did as the man suggested, taking a seat and perching her handbag on her lap as some kind of shield between them. He glanced at it as if he'd guessed its purpose and his lips tilted into a knowing smirk.

Feeling exposed under his steady gaze, she somehow defeated the urge to jump back up and leave. It wasn't as if she had many alternatives right now. After this bar she had nowhere to go except back to her hotel room, and then possibly back to Brooklyn. Defeated. She wouldn't do that. Ever.

'Like what you see?'

His deep voice slid over her skin like the richest velvet, making her realise that she'd been caught staring at his mouth. Alarmed, she realised that the tingly sensation swamping her senses was some sort of sexual attraction she couldn't remember ever experiencing before.

A betraying jolt went through her and his lazy, heavy-lidded gaze told her that he was too experienced to have missed it.

Flustered and appalled at her own lack of sense, she dragged her eyes to his. 'You speak English.'

'Evidently.'

His droll tone and imperious gaze made her feel even more stupid than she'd felt already, and she grimaced. 'I meant you speak English *well*.'

His only response was to raise one eyebrow in condescension. Regan got the distinct impression that he didn't like her. But how was that possible when she had never even met him before?

'What are you doing here, American?' His voice was low and rough, his lips curling with disdain.

No, he didn't like her. Not one little bit.

'How do you know I'm American? Are you?' She hadn't been able to place his accent yet.

He gave her a humourless smile. 'Do I look American to you?'

No, he looked like a man who could tempt a nun to relinquish her vows. And he knew it. 'No. Sorry.'

'So what are you doing here?'

She let out a breath and pulled herself together. She didn't know whether to hold the photo of Chad out to him or not. Despite his relaxed slouch, he looked as if he was ready to pounce on her if she so much as blinked the wrong way. 'I'm...looking for someone.'

'Someone?'

'My brother.' Deciding there couldn't be any harm in showing him the photo, she extended it across the table, making sure their fingers didn't connect when he took it. His eyes held hers for a fraction longer than necessary as if he knew exactly what she was thinking. Which she hoped wasn't true because she was still stuck on the whole sexual attraction thing. 'Have you seen him before?'

'Maybe. Why are you looking for him?'

Regan's eyes widened. Hope welled up inside her at the thought that she might have finally found someone who would be able to help her. 'You have? Where? When?'

'I repeat, why are you looking for him?'

'Because I don't know where he is. Do you?'

'When was the last time you heard from him?'

His tone was blunt. Commanding. And suddenly she felt as though he was the one looking for Chad instead of her.

'Why won't you answer my questions?' she asked, her instincts warning her to tread carefully.

'Why won't you answer mine?'

'I have.' She shifted uncomfortably in her seat. 'How do you know my brother?'

'I didn't say I knew him.'

'But you did...you said...' She shook her head. What exactly had he said? She lifted her hand to her head where it had started to ache. 'Look, if you don't know him just say so. I've had a long day and I'm really tired. Not that you care, I know, but if you know where he is I'd really appreciate you telling me.'

He looked at her for so long she didn't think he was going to say anything. 'I don't know where he is.'

Something in his tone didn't sound right but her brain was so foggy she couldn't pick up on what it was. All she could focus on was a growing despair. After the surge of hope she'd felt moments ago it seemed to weigh more heavily on her than it had all day. 'Okay, well—'

'When was the last time you heard from him?' he asked for a second time.

Regan paused before answering him. She didn't know this man from Adam. He didn't know her either for that matter. So why was he asking her so many questions? 'Why do you want to know that? You already said you don't know where he is.'

He shrugged his broad shoulders. 'I don't. But I didn't say I wouldn't help you.'

Their eyes clashed and Regan had a sudden image of a lethal mountain lion eyeing off a prairie rabbit. 'Help me?'

'Of course. You look like a woman who is almost out of options.'

She *was* a woman who was almost out of options. But how did he know that? Did she look as desperate as she felt?

He smiled at her but it held not a hint of warmth. 'Are you going to deny it?'

Regan's brows drew together. She wanted to deny it but she couldn't. And really she *could* use some help right now. Especially from someone who was a local and knew the area well. Someone who might even know Chad. But this man had already admitted that he didn't, and frankly he unsettled her. She'd thought he was dangerous when she'd first spotted him from across the room and, while closer inspection might have confirmed that he was incredibly good-looking, it hadn't shifted her initial impression one bit. Which was strange because he hadn't made a single threatening move towards her. Still, she listened to her instincts and there was something about him she didn't trust. 'Thanks anyway, but I'm good.'

'Good?' He gave a humorous laugh. 'You're a foreign woman in a bar, alone at night in a city you don't know. Exactly how are you good, America?'

She pursed her lips at both the nickname he had given her and the element of truth behind his words. When she'd first set out it had been early evening and she hadn't given much thought to the time. All she'd considered was finding information that might lead to Chad. But she wasn't completely vulnerable, was she? She had her mace. 'I just am. I'm from New York. I know what I'm doing.'

'Really? So what's your plan now? You going to go bar-hopping and hold up your little photo to every person you come across?' He made the only idea that had come into her head sound ridiculous. 'That's fine if you're looking for trouble as well as your brother.'

'I'm not looking for trouble,' she retorted hotly.

His gaze narrowed at her haughty tone, his inky black lashes making his blue eyes seem electric. It was totally unfair that she should have brown hair and brown eyes while this man was one of the most beautiful creatures she had ever seen in the flesh.

'Take a look outside. You have been in my country for less than twenty-four hours and you know nothing about it. You should be glad that I'm offering my assistance.'

Regan narrowed her eyes suspiciously. 'How do you know how long I've been in Santara?'

'Any longer and you would know not to swan into a bar in this part of town without an escort who could take on fifty men.'

Regan felt a trickle of unease roll down her spine. She glanced around the room to find it even busier than before. 'I'd like my photo back, please,' she said, standing to go.

He watched her, unmoving. 'Where are you going?'

As if she was silly enough to tell him that. 'I've taken up enough of your time,' she said briskly, 'and it's getting late.'

'So you're just going to turn around and walk out of here?'

'I am,' she said with more bravado than she felt. 'Do you have a problem with that?'

'I don't know, America; can you take on fifty men?'

Regan shivered at the husky note in his voice, her body responding to him in a way she really couldn't fathom. Their eyes clashed and something raw and elemental passed between them.

Again, he hadn't moved but she got the distinct impression that he was a bigger threat to her than fifty other men could ever be.

Not wanting to put that to the test, she gave him a tight smile. 'We'll have to see, won't we?'

Once more conversation slowed as curious eyes surveyed her and Regan stuck her hand in her bag, palming her can of mace, before turning and striding towards the entrance of the bar as if her life depended on it.

Relieved when she made it outside without incident, she sighed and hailed a cab that by some miracle pulled into the kerb in front of her.

'Hello? Are you free?' she asked the pleasant-looking driver wearing some sort of chauffeur's hat.

'Yes, miss.'

'Thank heavens.' She jumped in the back and gave the driver the name of her hotel, only feeling as though she could fully relax when the dark car started moving. Which was when she realised that the stranger in black hadn't given Chad's photo back to her.

She glanced out through the rear window, half expecting to find him standing on the pavement watching her, but of course he wasn't. She was being silly now. And the photo didn't matter. She would print off another one tomorrow.

CHAPTER TWO

JAG STOOD OUTSIDE the door to Regan James's hotel room and questioned the validity of his actions. He'd been doing that the whole drive over.

After meeting her in the bar it was clear that she knew nothing about her brother's whereabouts. She also seemed to know nothing about his sister being with him. But then she had grown cagey when he'd probed her about the last time her brother had contacted her, and he didn't know if that was because her sense of self-preservation had kicked in, or whether she had something to hide.

Regardless, she was his only link to Chad James and she would undoubtedly have a wealth of significant information about her brother that could lead him to find his sister.

A predatory stillness entered his body as he raised his hand to knock at the door. Regan James had been a revelation at the bar. He'd been right when he'd first seen her photo. Her eyes were not brown, they were cinnamon, and her hair was a russet gold that reminded him of the desert sands lit by the setting sun. Her voice had also been a revelation; a husky mixture of warmth and pure sex.

She had evidently reminded some of the other men in the bar of the same thing because Jag had noticed the sensual speculation in more than one male gaze as she had moved through the bar. She had a slender grace that drew the eye and her smile was nothing short of stunning. Even his own breathing had quickened at that first sight of her, and when she'd stood in front of his table, her doe eyes wide and uncertain, he'd had the shocking impulse to reach across the table and drag her into his lap.

It had been a long time since he'd responded to a woman with such unchecked desire and the only reason he was even here was because he'd realised that he couldn't interrogate her in the bar. As it was, some of his people had started to recognise him despite the fact that he'd shaved off his customary neat beard and moustache. He rubbed his hand across his clean-shaven jaw, quite liking the sensation of bare skin. Instantly the thought of rubbing his cheek along Regan

James's creamy décolletage entered his head and altered his breathing.

He scowled at the unruly thought. It had been a long time since he'd been influenced by his emotions rather than his intellect as well; some might have said never. Milena often accused him of having ice running through his veins, of being inhuman. He wasn't. He was as human as the next man, as his physical reaction to Regan James earlier had proven.

The fact was, Jag had learned to control his emotions at an early age and he didn't see anything wrong with that. As a leader it was essential that he keep a cool head when everyone else was losing theirs. He had certainly never let a pretty face or a sexy body influence his decision-making process and he never would.

Irritated that he was even pondering emotions and sex, he raised his fist to bang on the door.

He heard the sound of water being shut off and a feminine, 'Just a minute.'

He let out a rough breath. Excellent; she was just out of the shower.

The door opened wide and he found himself staring into Regan James's gorgeous eyes. Sec-

onds seemed to lengthen into minutes as his eyes
automatically travelled down her slender form.

'You!'

'Me,' Jaeger growled, his voice roughened by
the swift rise of his body at the sight of her in a
cotton dressing gown and towel around her head.
He pushed past her into the room before she had
a chance to collect herself and slam the door in
his face.

'Hold on. You can't come barging in here.'

Jag didn't bother to point out the obvious. That
he already had. Instead he scanned the small
room, looking for any signs that might clue him
in as to where her brother might be.

'Did you hear me?' She yanked on his arm to
turn him towards her and the move was so unexpected, so shocking that he did indeed turn towards her, a frown on his face. Nobody touched
him without first being given permission to do
so. Ever.

His eyes narrowed as she clutched the lapels
of her robe closed, making him acutely aware
that she was naked beneath the thin cloth. He
wanted nothing more than to wrench the gar-
ment from her body and sink into her feminine
softness until he couldn't remember what it felt

like to be burdened by duty. Until he couldn't remember what it felt like to be alone. But no one could escape destiny and one night in this woman's arms wouldn't change anything. Duty and loneliness went hand in hand. He'd learned that from watching his father.

Savagely tamping down on needs that had materialised from who knew where, he scowled at her.

'I heard you.'

'Then…' She lifted her chin in response to his brusqueness. 'What are you doing here?'

Jag glanced at the photo of her brother in his hand before flicking it onto the coffee table. 'You left this behind.'

Her gaze landed on the photo. 'Well…thanks for returning it, but you could have left it with the front desk downstairs.'

Ignoring her, Jag raised the flap of her suitcase and peered at the contents. 'Is this all the luggage you have?'

Frowning at him, she crossed the room and slammed it closed. 'That's none of your business.'

Deciding that he'd wasted enough time humouring this woman, Jag gave her a look that usually sent grown men into hiding. 'I asked you a question.'

This close, he dwarfed her in height and form, but her instincts for survival must have been truly lost because she still didn't move back from him.

'And I asked you to leave,' she shot back.

Jag's lip curled. He would have thought her much braver than she looked if not for that pulse point throbbing like a battering ram at the base of her neck.

'I'm not leaving.' His voice held a dark warning. 'Not before you've told me everything you know about your brother.'

'You do know my brother, don't you?' Finally she took a quick step backwards. 'Do you also know where he is? Did you lie about that?'

'I ask the questions. You answer them,' he stated coldly.

She shook her head. 'Who are you?'

'That is not important.'

'Do you have my brother?' Her voice held a fine tremor of panic. 'You do, don't you?'

Jag's lip curled into a snarl. 'If I had your brother, why would I be here?'

'I don't know.' Those cinnamon-brown eyes were riveted to his. 'I don't know what you want or why you're here.' She swallowed heavily and Jag felt his chest constrict at her obvious fear. The need to soothe it—the need to soothe her—took him completely by surprise.

Knowing this would go a lot easier if she were relaxed he tried for a conciliatory tone. 'There's no need to be afraid, Miss James. I merely want to ask you some questions.'

His saying her name seemed to jolt something loose inside of her. He saw the rise of panic in the way her eyes darted to the side, clearly searching out an avenue of escape. Before he could think of how to placate her, to put her at ease, she darted, quick as a whippet, towards the hotel room phone.

If he'd wanted to alert hotel security to his presence he'd have called them himself and he had no choice but to stop her, wrapping his arms around her from behind and lifting her bodily off the ground.

She fought him like a little cat with its tail caught in a door, her nails digging into his forearms, the towel around her head whipping him in the face before falling to the ground.

'Keep still,' Jag growled, wincing as her heel connected with his shin. For a little thing she had a lot of spunk in her and if he wasn't so irritated he'd be impressed. 'Dammit, I'm not—' Jag grunted out an expletive as her elbow came perilously close to connecting with his groin.

Deciding to put an end to her thrashing, he spun her around to face him and gripped her hands behind her back, bringing her body into full contact with his. Her flimsy robe had become dislodged during the struggle and this new position put her barely constrained breasts flat up against the wall of his chest. His traitorous body registered the impact and responded as if it belonged to a fifteen-year-old youth rather than a thirty-year-old man who was also a king.

She panted as she glared up at him, her wet hair wild around her flushed face. Jag's breath stalled. Like this, with her cheeks flushed, her lips parted, her breathing ragged, she looked absolutely magnificent. And that was *absolutely* irrelevant.

'I'm going to put you down,' he said carefully. 'If you run again, or go for the weapon in your handbag, I'll restrain you. If you stay put this will be a lot easier.'

For him at least.

Her fulminating glare told him she didn't believe him, but at least she'd stopped struggling.

He shook his head when she remained stubbornly silent and released her anyway. He was twice her size; if she ran again he'd stop her again. Only he'd prefer not to. It was most likely due to the stress of his sister's disappearance, but being this close to Regan James was playing havoc with his senses.

'Where is your phone?'

He'd check to see if she'd received any calls during the day and move on from there. He glanced into her angry face when she didn't immediately answer. By the set of her jaw she had no intention of doing so.

'Miss James, do not infuriate me again by making this more difficult than it has to be.'

'Infuriate you! That's rich! You follow me to my hotel, barge into my room and then attack me. And you're the one who's infuriated?'

'I did not attack you,' Jag said with all the patience of a saint. 'I restrained you and I will do so again if you run again. Be warned.'

She folded her arms across her chest, a shiver

racing down her body. 'What do you want?' She lifted her chin at a haughty angle.

'Not you,' he grated, 'so you can rest easy about that.'

She looked at him as if she didn't believe him and he could hardly blame her after the way he'd handled her. Still, it was true. He preferred his lovers sophisticated, compliant and willing. She was none of those three. So why was he so affected by her?

'Take a seat,' he growled, 'so we can get down to what it is that I do want. Which is information about your brother.'

When she remained stubbornly standing Jag sighed and sat himself.

'A week ago your brother wrote to you. Have you spoken to him since?'

'How do you know he wrote to me?'

'I ask the questions, Miss James,' he reminded her with forced patience. 'You answer them.'

'I'm not telling you anything.'

'I would seriously advise you to reconsider that approach.' His voice was steely soft. She might not know it but there wasn't anything he wouldn't do to find his sister, and the reminder that this woman's brother had her reignited his anger. She looked at him as if she wanted to bite him and he felt another unbidden surge of lust hit him hard.

'No, I haven't heard from him,' she finally bit out.

'What made you come to Santara?'

Her lips compressed and for a moment he thought she might defy him again. 'Because he lives here. And I was worried when he didn't answer his cell phone.'

'He did live here.' He wasn't going to for much longer.

She shook her head. 'He wouldn't move without telling me.'

'I take it you're close.'

'Very.'

The soft conviction in her voice jolted something loose inside his chest. He had once been that close to his own siblings. Then his father had died in a light-aircraft crash that had made him King. There hadn't been time for closeness after that. There hadn't been *room* for it.

'What do you know about what your brother has been up to lately?'

'Nothing.'

'Really?' He watched the flush of guilt rise along her neck with satisfaction.

'I don't,' she said, shifting from one foot to the other, her eyes flashing fire and brimstone at him as she fought her desire to defy him. He would have been amused if he didn't find her audacity so invigorating. So arousing.

'I mean, I know that he was enjoying work, that he liked to explore the countryside on weekends, that he had just bought a new toaster oven he was particularly proud of, and that he had a new assistant.'

'A new assistant?'

'Yes. Look, I'm not answering any more of your questions until you answer mine.' She planted her hands on her hips, inadvertently widening the neck of her robe. 'Why are you so interested in my brother?'

Dragging his gaze up from her shadowy cleavage, he savagely tamped down on his persistent libido. 'He has something of mine.' His jaw clenched as he wondered how Milena was. Whether she was okay, or if she was in trouble. If she needed him.

'He stole from you?'

The shock in her voice pulled his mouth into a grim slash. 'You could say that.'

* * *

Regan noted the subtle shift in his muscles when he answered her, the coiled tension that clenched his jaw and his fists at the same time. Again she thought of a mountain lion ready to spring. Whatever her brother had taken it was important to this man. And that, at least, explained his interest in Chad. But, while her brother had gone through a couple of rough years after their parents died, he wasn't a bad person. He was smart, much smarter than her, which was why she had worked so hard to make sure he finished high school, finally fulfilling his potential with a university degree in AI at the top of his class. An achievement that had brought him to this country that was, from the little she had seen, both untamed and beautiful.

Much like the stranger in front of her who left her breathless whenever he trained his blue gaze on her as if he was trying to see inside her. Possibly she hated that most of all; the way her body responded to his with just a look.

He was watching her now and it took all her concentration to ignore the sensations spiralling through her. If he hadn't touched her before, grabbed her and held her hard against him it might have been easier.

Regan's nipples tightened at the memory of his arm brushing over her. He was built like a rock, all hard dips and plains that had been a perfect foil for her own curves. And she was in a hotel room alone with him. A man who outweighed her by about a hundred pounds.

'It wasn't Chad,' she said fiercely, forcing her mind back on track.

'It was.'

'My brother isn't a thief,' she said with conviction. 'You've made a mistake.'

'I don't have the luxury of making mistakes in my line of work. Which I have to get back to. Where's your phone?'

'Why do you want my phone?'

Thick black lashes narrowed so that the blue of his eyes was almost completely concealed. 'I've humoured you enough, Miss James. Where is it?'

He uncoiled from the sofa, all latent, angry male energy, and she instinctively stepped back. He noticed, causing her temper to override her anxiety. 'First tell me who you are. You owe me at least that for scaring the life out of me before.'

'Actually I don't owe you anything, America.'

His gaze travelled over her with blatant male appraisal. 'I am the King of Santara, Sheikh Jaeger Salim al-Hadrid.'

'The King?' Regan clapped a hand over her mouth to stifle a laugh. The man might have an expensive-looking haircut, now that she could see it without the headdress he'd worn earlier, but with his dark clothing and scuffed boots he looked more like a mercenary than a king. And then another thought struck. Had he been hired to kill Chad? Did he think she would inadvertently lead him to her brother? 'I doubt that. Who are you really?'

She saw instantly that laughing at this man was the wrong thing to do. His blue gaze pinned her to the spot, his body going hunting-still. 'I am the King,' he said coldly, taking a step towards her.

'Okay, okay.' Regan held her hand out to ward him off. 'I believe you.' She didn't but he didn't need to know that. As long as he left—and soon—that was all she needed him to do.

She forced her brain to forget about the perfect symmetry of his face and start thinking more about surviving. He was clearly a madman—or a potential killer—and she was alone with him in her room.

Fresh fear spiked along her spine. She tried to remember that everyone said she had a gift for communicating but this was no recalcitrant seven-year-old with a smartphone hidden beneath his desk.

'You think I'm lying?' he said softly.

'No, no.' Regan rushed to assure him, only to have him bark out a harsh sound that was possibly laughter.

'Unbelievable.'

He shook his head and Regan briefly measured the distance from her to the door.

'Too far,' he murmured, as if reading her mind. Probably not difficult, since she was staring at the door as if she was willing it to open by itself. Which she was.

'Look—'

He moved so quickly she barely got one word out before he was in front of her. 'No more questions. No more games. Give me your phone or I'll tear everything apart until I find it.'

'Bathroom.'

His eyes narrowed.

'I was taking a shower when you turned up,' she said. 'I like to play music while I'm in there.'

'Get it.'

Nearly demanding that he say 'please', Regan decided that the best thing she could do was to stay quiet. The sooner he got what he was looking for, the sooner he would leave.

Moving on wooden legs, she walked towards the bathroom, coming up short when he followed her. Staring back at him in the bathroom mirror, she saw just how big he was, his wide shoulders filling the doorway and completely blocking out the view of the room behind him.

Their eyes connected and for a brief moment awareness charged the air between them, turning her hot. Flustered, she dropped her eyes and picked up her phone. She handed it to him, crossing her arms over her chest in a purely protective gesture.

'Password?'

Heat radiated from his body, surrounding her, and she wished he'd move back. 'Trudyjack,' she said grudgingly.

'Your parents' names?' He gave her a bemused look. 'You might as well have used ABC.'

Regan's eyes flashed to his. How did he know they were her parents' names? *How did he know so much about her?*

'Who are you?' she whispered, frightened all over again.

'I told you. I am the King of Santara. I knew everything about you less than an hour after your plane landed in my country.'

Regan swallowed hard and pressed herself against the basin behind her. Could he really be who he said he was? It didn't seem possible, and yet he did have an unmistakable aura of power and authority about him. But then so did killers, she imagined.

She watched him scroll through her contact list and emails, his scowl darkening in the lengthening silence.

'Chad's phone is switched off,' she said, unable to keep her vow of silence from moments ago. She couldn't help it. She'd never been good with silences and when she was nervous that only became worse. 'I know because I've tried to call him daily.'

'He doesn't have his phone with him.'

'Then what are you searching for on my phone?'

'A burner number. An email from an unknown source.'

'How do you know he doesn't have it with him?'

Ignoring her question, he asked another one of his own. 'Does he have a second phone?'

Regan frowned. Why would Chad not take his phone with him? His phone was his lifeline. 'No. But I wouldn't tell you even if he did.'

His blue eyes melded with hers, a zing of heat landing low in her belly.

'You like to provoke me, don't you, Miss James?'

Regan's heart skipped a beat at his warning tone. No, she didn't like to provoke him. She really didn't.

With a look of disgust he pocketed her phone. She wanted to tell him that he couldn't keep it because her phone was her lifeline too, but at this point she'd do almost anything to placate him and make him go away.

'Satisfied?' she asked, the word husky on her lips.

'Hardly.' His gaze raked down over her again and she became acutely aware of her nudity beneath her robe. The small room seemed to shrink even more and the air grew heavy between them, making it nearly impossible for her to breathe. The man had a dire effect on her system, there was no question about that.

'Why were you so keen to jump on a plane and fly here after that one email?'

'I...' Regan swallowed. 'I was worried. It's not like Chad to be out of contact.'

'So you rushed over here because you thought he might be in trouble? Do you always put your brother first, or is it that you like to feel indispensable?'

Regan's pride jolted at his words because there was some truth to them. Becoming Chad's guardian and throwing herself into the role had helped to fill a void in her life and move on from her grief.

Hot colour flamed in her face. 'You don't know me.'

'Nor do I want to. Get dressed,' he ordered before turning and walking back into the main room.

Regan exhaled, willing herself to be calm. She moved to the doorway to find him going through the photos on her camera. Instantly she went into panic mode. 'Hey, don't touch that. It's old and I can't afford to replace it.'

She lunged to retrieve her precious camera and he held it aloft. 'I'm not going to break it,' he snapped. 'Not unless you keep trying to grab it.'

Snatching her hand back from where it had landed on the hard ball of his shoulder, she slapped her hands on her hips. 'I don't care who you are, you have no right to go through my things.'

He gave her a dismissive glance to say that he had every right and even if he didn't there wasn't a damned thing she could do about it. 'There isn't anything I won't do to get my sister back, Miss James. You'd better get used to that idea.'

His sister?

Regan frowned. 'What has your sister got to do with anything?'

Slowly his gaze returned to hers, the blue so clear and so cold she could have been staring into a glacier. 'Your brother has my sister. And now I have his.'

'That's insane.'

'For once we agree on something.'

'No, I mean you're insane. My brother isn't with your sister. He would have told me.'

'Really?'

Maybe. Maybe not. 'Are they in a relationship or something?' If they were she was a bit hurt that he hadn't told her. They had always shared everything in the past.

'You'd better hope not. Now move. My patience is at an end. I need to return to the palace.'

Wait? Was he really the King of Santara?

'I'm… I'm not going anywhere with you.'

'If you insist on going as you are I won't stop you. But you'll get far more looks than you did earlier, parading around in tight jeans and a flimsy shirt.'

'My clothes were perfectly respectable, thank you very much.'

'You have five minutes.'

'I'm not going with you.'

'That's your choice, of course, but the alternative is that you remain in this room until your brother returns.'

Regan frowned. 'You mean as in *locked* in here?'

'I can't afford to have my sister's disappearance become public knowledge. With you asking questions and wandering around on your own you'll only draw attention to yourself. And, no doubt, get yourself into trouble in the process.'

'I won't say anything. I promise!'

Regan knew she sounded desperate and she was. The thought of being locked in a hotel room for who knew how long was not acceptable. If what this man said was true she wanted freedom to find Chad and figure out what was going on. Preferably before this man found him.

He shook his head. 'Make your decision. I don't have all night.'

'I'm not staying here!'

'Then get dressed.'

Regan's mind was spinning out of control. Her head, already fuzzy from lack of sleep, was struggling to keep pace with the rate at which things were moving. 'I need more time to think about this.'

'I gave you five minutes. You now have four.'

'I don't think I've ever met a more arrogant person than you. Actually, strike that: I know I haven't.'

He folded his hands across his chest, his muscular legs braced wide, his expression hard. Like this he looked as if he could take on fifty men blindfolded and win.

'Your telephone service will be disconnected and I will have guards posted outside your door. I do not advise you to try to leave.'

'But how do I know you are who you say you are?' she said on a rush. 'You could be an imposter for all I know. A murderer. I'd be crazy to go with you.'

'I am not a murderer.'

'I don't know that!'

'Get dressed and I'll prove it to you.'

'How?'

He heaved an impatient sigh. 'You can ask any member of the hotel staff downstairs. They will know who I am.'

For the first time since he had barged into her room Regan saw a way out. If he was really going to take her downstairs then she had a chance of alerting someone as to what was going on.

'Okay, just…' She grabbed a clean pair of jeans and a long-sleeved shirt from her case. 'Just give me a minute.'

Locking herself in the bathroom, she very nearly didn't come back out but decided that he'd most likely break the door down if she aggravated him too much. He had the arms for it.

Concentrating more on his abundant negative qualities, she opened the door to find him propping up the opposite wall, looking at his watch. 'One minute early. I'm impressed.'

Arrogant jerk.

Regan grabbed her handbag and walked ahead

of him out the door. She waited as he stabbed the elevator button. 'If you're really a king, where are all your guards?'

'I rarely take guards with me on unofficial business. I can take care of myself.'

Convenient, she thought.

'And why was it that no one in the shisha bar knew your identity? If you're really the King I would have expected some bowing and scraping.'

The slow smile he gave her told her he wouldn't mind making her bow and scrape for him. 'I've found that people rarely see what they're least expecting.'

Regan raised a brow. She couldn't argue with that. She might have thought he looked dangerous when she had first seen him, but she hadn't expected him to turn up at her door making outrageous accusations about her brother. Nor had she expected him to tell her he was the King. Though whether or not that was true still remained to be seen.

'How's the headache?' he asked, watching her in the mirrored wall. Regan slid her gaze to his. 'Don't bother denying it,' he continued. 'You're so pale you look like you're about to pass out.'

'My head is fine.' She wasn't about to admit

that he was right. She wasn't sure what he would do with the information. She wouldn't put it past him to try to make it worse.

When they arrived at the lobby Regan felt a surge of adrenaline race through her. Glancing around, she was disappointed to find that the large lobby was mostly empty. Before she could make a move in either direction her arm was gripped, vice-like, and she was towed along towards the reception desk.

The smile on the young man's face faltered as he took them in. They probably looked quite a sight, she thought grimly. Her with her fast-drying hair no doubt resembling a wavy cloud around her head, and her unwanted companion with a scowl as dark as his clothing.

'Ah, Your Majesty, it is an honour.' The man bowed towards the desk, his expression one of eternal deference. Then he said something in Santarian that her companion answered. The younger man's eyes went as big and as round as a harvest moon.

'But…' He gave her a panicked look. 'Miss James, this is His Majesty the King of Santara.' The words almost came out in a stutter, as if he couldn't quite believe he was saying them.

Frankly, nor could Regan. 'How do I know you haven't just set this up?' she said with disdain. 'One man's opinion is hardly folk law.' Turning back to the concierge, Regan said, 'Actually, I'd like to report—'

She didn't get any further as the stranger beside her growled something low under his breath and then towed her further into the lobby, veering off towards the sound of a pianist playing a soulful song. Through French windows Regan saw a room full of people.

Stopping just inside the entrance, they stood waiting until finally most of the room grew silent, staring at the two of them. Then half of the occupants stood and bowed low towards the man still holding her arm.

Regan shook her head, her brain refusing to compute the evidence that he really was the King of Santara. Which meant that if he was right then maybe her brother was with his sister, *Princess* Milena, his new research assistant. She swallowed, swaying on her feet.

Clearly worried she was about to do something girly, like swoon in his presence, the King snaked a hand around her waist, pulling her up against him. Regan set her hand flat against his chest to stop their bodies colliding. Her head fell back on the stem of her neck as the heat from his body sapped the last of her strength. She could feel his heart pounding a steady rhythm to match her own but all she could focus on was the blue of his eyes, indigo in the soft light. Time seemed to disappear as he looked back at her with such heat Regan's thoughts ceased to exist. It didn't matter who she was or what he was. All that mattered was that he kiss her. Kiss her so that the ache building inside her subsided.

A soft growl left his throat, his eyes devouring her lips, and for a brief moment she thought he *would* kiss her.

But then his eyes turned as sharp as chipped jewels and his hand tightened on her hip. 'Satisfied?' he murmured, throwing her earlier question back at her.

Regan shook her head, her balance precarious despite his firm hold. She heard the word 'no' coming from a long, dark tunnel right before she did something she'd never done before. She fainted.

CHAPTER THREE

TWO NIGHTS LATER Jag sat behind his large desk brooding over the voice message he had received from Milena.

'Hi Jag. I know you're worried—you're you— and I'm sorry I can't tell you where I am, or what I'm doing, but I want you to know that I'm with a friend and I'm fine. I'll explain everything when I return. I love you.'

'Any idea where the call originated from?' he asked Tarik.

'Unfortunately not. It was likely made from a burner phone and it was sent through several different carriers. Whoever scrambled the transmission is good.'

Chad had scrambled the transmission, of that Jag was one hundred percent certain; he'd hired the kid in the first place because he was a borderline genius with technology. Anger coursed through him, a hot and welcome replacement for the impotence he'd felt since she'd gone.

He turned to stare outside the window, brooding. On the one hand he was happy that his sister was safe and well, but the reality was that she could have been forced into making that phone call. Not that she'd sounded forced. She'd sounded full of vigour. Almost buoyant. A state he hadn't seen her in for quite a while. A state he would welcome if the memory of what had transpired three years ago wasn't like a smoking gun in his mind.

Then there was the obvious assumption that if she hadn't been forced to leave Santara then she'd gone somewhere with Chad James of her own free will, and that raised a whole host of ugly questions Jag didn't want to consider. Questions like, what were they doing together that Milena wasn't able to tell him about? Like maybe she was considering not going through with the marriage to the Crown Prince of Toran? Questions like, was she unhappy, and, if so, why hadn't she come to him the way she used to when she was a child?

He rubbed his fingers hard across his forehead. Well, of course she'd been coerced. There was no other way to look at this. Just as he had coerced Regan James into coming to the palace. He recalled the moment she had fainted when she had discovered that he was actually the King, the dead weight of her body as she'd slumped in his arms. He'd had a lot of reactions from women in the past when they'd found out he was royalty— everything from obsequious preening to outright manipulation—but he'd never had a woman faint on him before. Which had been a good thing because right before that he'd nearly given in to an urge he'd been fighting all night and leant down and kissed her. In public! He didn't know what bothered him about that the most: the fact that his inimitable self-control had taken a long hike, or that he would have shocked the hell out of those watching.

Shocked himself, he'd quickly scooped her into his arms and taken her out to his waiting SUV. She'd come to fairly quickly in the car, demanding that he return her to her hotel, but he had calmly reminded her that it had been her choice to come with him and that she was now out of options.

Well aware that his behaviour had been less than stellar with regard to the American woman, he pushed thoughts of her, and his sister, from his head and picked up the raft of reports he needed to sign off. 'These can go to Helen to have the corrections worked up, these can go back to Finance, and this one I still have to read. Tell Ryan I'll get to it later tonight.'

'Very good.'

He rubbed the back of his neck. 'For once I hope that's it for the night.' He gave Tarik a faint smile and saw the old man hesitate. It was only the slightest of movements but Jag knew him too well to miss it. His body immediately shifted into combat mode. 'What is it? And please tell me it has nothing to do with the American.'

As much as he had been trying to keep her presence in the palace under wraps, she had been trying to stop him. Banging on the door of her suite, demanding that she be given her phone and her computer, demanding that she be released, demanding that he come to her. But Jag didn't want to go to her. Already her voice and the memory of her scent had imprinted themselves on his brain. He couldn't imagine that seeing her was going to make that any better.

'Unfortunately it does. She is refusing to eat,' Tarik said.

'Refusing to eat?' Jaeger felt his stomach knot. 'Since when?'

'Since last night, sir. She did not eat her evening meal and today she has rejected all food.'

Jag's jaw hardened. If Regan thought she was going to make herself ill by not eating she had another thing coming.

Trying not to overreact, he pushed himself to his feet. 'What time is her evening meal due to be delivered?'

'It has been delivered. She sent it away.'

Jaeger scowled. 'Have my dinner taken to her suite in half an hour.'

He made to leave but again Tarik hesitated.

'Please tell me you've left the best to last,' Jag drawled.

Tarik grimaced. 'Not exactly, Your Majesty, but I have it in hand.' He passed Jaeger a printout from a local news website. On it were two photos of himself and Regan standing close together. They must have been snapped by one of the patrons in the hotel, the camera perfectly capturing the moment she had discovered he was the King: her eyes wide, lips softly parted, wild mane cascading down her back like a silken waterfall. The next was right before she'd fainted. Jag had tangled his fingers through her hair to cup the nape of her neck, his other hand tight around her waist. Her face had been upturned, her mouth inches from his own. Would those pink lips have tasted as pure and sweet as they looked? Would the skin of her abdomen feel as soft beneath his fingertips as the nape of her neck? Would—?

Tarik cleared his throat. Jag inhaled deeply, uncomfortably aware that his trousers were fitting a little snugger than they were before. What the hell was wrong with him?

'Fortunately they were taken down before any damage was done,' Tarik informed him. 'And the woman's name was not discovered. But I thought you should be informed.'

'Of course I should be informed.' He glanced at the images again, an idea forming in his mind at rapid speed. If he was going to detain Regan James until her brother returned then by damned he would make her useful to him. 'Republish the photos.'

'Your Majesty?'

'Make sure her name is attached and that the images are picked up by the international Press. If the sight of her in my arms doesn't bring her brother out of the woodwork, I don't know what will.'

Tarik looked at him as if he wanted to protest

but Jag wasn't in the mood to listen. He wanted a hot meal, a cool shower and a peaceful night's sleep. Since meeting her the American woman had interfered with the latter; now it seemed she would be interfering with the first two as well.

Regan's stomach grumbled loudly in the silent room and she pressed her palm against her belly. 'It's been one day,' she told her objectionable organ. 'People can survive a lot longer than that without food, so stop complaining.'

She didn't know exactly how long a human being could survive without food, but she recalled various movies about survival and knew it was more than a day.

Mind you she was starving and her errant brain advised her that food would help to keep her strength up. And that the arrogant ruler of Santara wouldn't care about her eating habits anyway.

But it wasn't just the lack of food bothering her. It was the boredom and worry. She'd come to Santara to make sure Chad was okay. Not only was she not doing that but she wasn't doing anything at all. She'd never had so much time on her hands and she was going crazy. The first day she had kept herself busy taking photos of the amazing garden suite she was imprisoned in; the arched Moorish windows, the Byzantine blues and greens that were used to colour the room and the amazing studded teak doors, the one keeping her locked in being the most beautiful of all, which she refused to see as ironic in any way.

Then there was the garden with the swaying palm trees, and deep blue tiled pool. The whole place was stunning and she itched to download her images onto her laptop and play around with the lighting and composition. If she'd been in this magical place under any other circumstances she doubted she'd want to leave.

But more than that she wanted to see the King again. Not because she wanted to see him per se, but because she wanted to know if he had an update on Chad. She hadn't realised when she'd made the choice to leave her hotel room that she'd be swapping one prison for another. Perhaps if she hadn't been so tired and strung-out, if he'd given her more time to consider her options, she would have made a different choice. She certainly wouldn't have thought about what it would feel like to kiss him!

She groaned softly in mortification as she recalled the moment he'd held her against him in the hotel lobby, the moment he'd held her inside her hotel room, his hot eyes on her cleavage, their bodies melded together so tightly she was convinced she'd felt... *Don't go there*, she warned herself. Bad enough that she'd recounted those times second by second in her dreams. The man might be stunningly attractive, but he was holding her against her will and accusing her brother of a terrible crime.

A crime she was even more convinced, now that she'd had some sleep, that he would never commit. If only that blasted King would give her the time of day so she could explain that to him. Explain what a gentle soul her brother was. Explain that Chad was the type to save baby birds in their back garden, not stomp on them.

When her brother had finished university and taken the prestigious opening at GeoTech Industries she'd thought her days of worrying about him had come to an end.

She'd been eighteen when their parents died and she'd been thrust into the role of parent. And she'd thought she'd done okay. But if Chad really had run off with the King's sister... She rubbed at her bare forearms, chilled despite the humid warmth of the night air. She couldn't take the King's claim seriously. Chad just wouldn't do something like that, she knew it. She knew him!

Sensing more than hearing a presence behind her, Regan slowly turned to find the man who had taken her captive standing in her living area. Her heart skipped a beat before taking off at a gallop. He looked magnificent in a white robe that enhanced his olive skin and blue eyes to perfection. He wasn't wearing a headdress tonight, his black hair thick and a little mussed from where it looked as though he had dragged his fingers through it countless times during the day. The glow from the elaborate overhead chandeliers threw interesting light and shadows over his face, making him even more handsome than she remembered.

'Miss James.'

Her name was like thick, rich treacle on his lips and she shivered, hiding her unwanted reaction by stepping forward. 'So you've finally decided to show up,' she grouched, instinct advising her that attack was the best form of defence with a man like this. 'How kind of you.'

He gave her a faint smile. 'I understand you're not eating.'

A small thrill of satisfaction shot through her. So her self-imposed starvation had worked. 'Yes. And I won't until you release me.'

He shrugged one broad shoulder as if to say that his care factor couldn't be lower. 'That's your choice. You won't die.'

'How do you know?' she shot back.

'It takes three weeks for a person to starve to death. You're in no danger yet.'

Resenting his sense of superiority, Regan frowned as he clapped his hands together and two servants wheeled a dining cart into the room. One by one they set an array of platters on the dining table near the window.

'Will that be all, Your Majesty?'

'For now.'

Regan gave him a look as they bowed and exited the room. 'Don't expect that clapping trick to work with me,' she warned. 'I'm not one of your minions.'

His silky gaze drifted over her and she wished she were wearing more than a pair of shorts and a T-shirt. If she'd thought he might actually show up she'd have pulled a curtain from the wall and draped herself in it. Anything so that she didn't feel so exposed.

'No, that would take far more optimism than even I have for that to occur.'

He moved to the dining table and took a seat, inspecting the array of stainless-steel dishes the servers had laid out.

'No matter what you say,' she advised him, 'I won't eat.'

He gave her a long-suffering look. 'Believe it or not, Miss James, I do not wish for you to have a bad experience during your stay in the palace. I even hoped that we might be…friends.'

'Friends?'

He shrugged. 'Acquaintances, then.'

Regan couldn't have been more incredulous if he'd suggested they take a spaceship to Mars. 'And you say you're not optimistic.' She scoffed. 'The only thing I want from you is for you to release me.'

'I can't do that. I already told you that I will do whatever it takes to have my sister returned home safely.'

'Just as I would do whatever it takes to have my brother returned home safely as well.'

He inclined his head, a reluctant smile tugging at the corners of his mouth. 'On this we understand each other.'

Not wanting to have anything in common with the man, Regan set him straight. 'What I understand is that you're an autocratic, stubborn, overbearing tyrant.'

He didn't respond to her litany of his faults and she narrowed her eyes as he uncovered the small platters of delicious-smelling food. His imperviousness to her only made her temper flare hotter.

Then her stomach growled, making her feel even more irritable. She watched him scoop up a dip with a piece of flatbread, his eyes on her the whole time. His tongue came out to lick at the corner of his mouth and a tremor went through her. 'You look ridiculous when you eat,' she lied. 'Can't you do that somewhere else?'

Expecting him to become angry with her, she was shocked when he laughed. 'You know, your disposition might be improved if you stopped denying yourself your basic needs. Hunger strikes are very childish.'

Stung to be called childish, Regan stared down at him. 'My disposition will only improve when you release me and stop saying awful things about my brother.'

His eyes narrowed when she mentioned Chad, but other than that he didn't show an ounce of emotion; instead he scooped up more food with his fingers and tempted her with it.

Irritated, she thought about moving outside but then decided against it. If he was going to antagonise her she would do the same back.

'You cannot think to stick with this plan,' she said, wandering closer to him.

Curious blue eyes met hers. 'What plan?'

'The one to keep me here until my brother returns with your sister.'

He leaned back in his chair, wiping his mouth with his napkin. As he regarded her Regan's eyes drifted over the hard planes of his face, those slashing eyebrows and his surly, oh, so sinful mouth. He would photograph beautifully, she thought. All that dominant masculine virility just waiting to be harnessed... It gave a girl the shivers. She could picture him astride a horse, outlined against the desert dunes with the sun at his muscled back. Or asleep on soft rumpled sheets, his muscular arms supporting his head, his powerful thighs—

Regan frowned. Sometimes her creative side was a real pain.

'Is that my plan?' His deep voice held a smooth superiority that set her teeth on edge.

'Well, obviously. But I already told you that I wouldn't say anything about your sister being missing. I'm even willing to sign something to say that I won't.'

'But how do I know I can trust you?'

'Because I'm a very trustworthy person. Call my boss. She'll tell you. I never say anything I don't mean or do anything I say I won't.'

'Admirable.'

'Don't patronise me.' She gripped the back of the carved teak dining chair opposite him. The smell of something delicious wafted into her sinuses and she nearly groaned. 'You're really horrible, you know that?'

'I've been called worse.'

'I don't doubt it. Oh…' She clenched her aching stomach as it moaned again, and glared at him. 'You did this on purpose, didn't you?'

'Did what?' he asked innocently.

'Brought food in here. You're trying to make me so hungry that I'll eat despite myself. Well, it won't work.' She glared into his sapphire-blue eyes. 'You can't break me.'

She wheeled away from the table, intending to spend the rest of the night in the garden until he left, but she didn't make it two steps before he stopped her, wrapping his arm around her waist and hauling her against him.

Regan let out a cry of annoyance and banged her fists down on his forearms.

'Stop doing that,' she demanded. Already her skin felt hot, her unreliable senses urging her to turn in his arms and press up against him. 'I hate it when you touch me.'

'Then stop defying me,' he grated in her ear, yanking the chair she'd just been gripping out from the table and dumping her in it.

'You like doing that, don't you?' she accused, rubbing her bottom to erase the impression left behind from being welded to his hard stomach. 'Using your brute strength to get what you want.'

He picked up his fork and pointed it at her. 'Eat. Before I really lose my temper and ask the palace doctor to get a tube and feed you that way.'

'You wouldn't dare.'

The smile on his face said he would, and that he'd enjoy it.

'I'm only doing this because now that I know you won't let me go I'm going to need my strength to escape,' she said, snatching up a delicate pastry from a silver platter and shoving it into her mouth. It dissolved with flaky deliciousness on her tongue, making her reach for another. She murmured appreciatively and blushed when she found him staring at her. 'What?' she grouched. 'Isn't this what you wanted all along?'

'Yes.' His voice was deep and low, and turned her insides to liquid.

Not wanting him to know just how much he affected her, she decided to take another tack. 'This is preposterous, you know?'

He glanced at her. 'The food? My chef will not be pleased to hear that.'

'Keeping me here.' She picked up her fork and stabbed at something delicious looking. 'It's the twenty-first century and you appear to be an educated man.' Though that was popular opinion, not hers. 'A ruler, for heaven's sake. You can't just impose your will on others whenever you feel like it.'

He gave a short bark of laughter. 'Actually I can.' He piled more food onto his plate. 'And I am aware of the century. But in my country the King creates the laws, which pretty much gives me carte blanche to do what I want, whenever I want.'

'That can't be true.' She frowned. 'You must

have checks and balances. A government of some sort.'

'I have a cabinet that helps me govern, if that's what you mean.'

'And what's their job? To rubber-stamp whatever you say?'

'Not quite.'

'They must be able to order you to let me go.'

'Not quite.'

Completely exasperated, Regan put down her fork. 'Look, you're making a big mistake here. I know my brother is innocent.'

His eyes narrowed on hers. 'We've had this conversation. Eat.'

'I can't. The conversation is killing my appetite.'

'Then stop talking.'

'God, you're impossible. Tell me, what makes you think that my brother has taken your sister? Because it's not something my brother would do. He's not a criminal.'

'He stole a car when he was sixteen and copies of his finals exams when he was seventeen.'

'Both times the charges were dropped,' she defended. 'And how do you even know this? Those files are closed because he was a minor.'

He gave her a look and she rolled her eyes. 'Right, you know everything.' She took a deep breath and let it out slowly. 'Chad got into the wrong crowd with the car thing and he stole the exam papers to sell them to help me out financially. We had a hot-water system to replace in our house and no money. He didn't need to steal the exams for himself. He's a straight-A student. Anyway, that's a lot different from *kidnapping* someone,' she shot at him.

'To say that you've been kidnapped is a trifle dramatic. You came to my country of your own free will. Now you are being detained because you're a threat to my sister's security.'

'I had nothing to do with your sister's disappearance!'

'No, but your brother did,' he pointed out silkily, 'and as you've already confirmed he has the capability for criminal activity.'

'He was young and he was going through a hard time,' she cried. 'That doesn't mean he's a career criminal.'

'Why was he having a hard time?'

'I'm surprised you don't know,' she mumbled; 'you seem to know everything else.'

He handed her a warm triangle of pastry. 'I

know that your parents both died of cancer seven weeks apart. Is that what you're referring to?'

'Yes.' Emotion tightened her chest. 'Chad was only fourteen at the time. It hit him hard and he didn't really grieve properly… I think it caught up with him.'

'That must have been hard to have both parents struck down by such a terrible disease. I'm sorry.'

'Thank you.' She shook her head and bit into the food he'd handed her, closing her eyes at the exquisite burst of flavours on her tongue. 'This is delicious. What is it?'

'It is called a *bureek*, a common delicacy in our region.' He frowned as he dragged his eyes up from her mouth. 'Who looked after the two of you when your parents died?'

'I was eighteen,' she said, unconsciously lifting her chin. 'I deferred my photography studies, got a job and took care of us both.'

He frowned. 'You had no other family who could take you in?'

'We had grandparents who lived across the country, and an aunt and uncle we saw on occasion, but they only had room for Chad and neither one of us wanted to be parted.'

His blue eyes studied her for a long time, then

he handed her another morsel of food. She took it, completely unprepared for his next words. 'I lost my father when I was nineteen.'

'Oh, I'm sorry,' she said instinctively. She missed her parents every day and her heart went out to him. 'How did he die?'

'He was killed in a helicopter crash.'

'Oh that's awful. What happened to you?'

'I became King.'

'At nineteen? But that's so young.'

He handed her another type of pastry. 'I was born to lead. For me it wasn't an issue.'

Wasn't an issue?

Regan stared at him. He might say it wasn't an issue but she knew how hard it was to take on the responsibility of one brother, let alone an entire country. 'It couldn't have been easy. Did you have time to mourn him at least?'

She noticed a flicker of surprise behind his steady gaze. 'I was studying in America when his light aircraft went down. By the time I arrived home the country was in turmoil. There were things to be done. Try the *manakeesh*.' He indicted the food she forgot she was holding. 'I think you'll like it.'

That would be a no, then, she thought, biting into a delicious mixture of bread, spice and mince. His slight grin told her he knew that she'd enjoyed it. She shook her head, trying to make sense of their conversation.

He might sound as if he were talking about little more than a walk in the park, but Regan could tell by the slight tightening of the skin around his eyes that his father's death had affected him very deeply. 'How old was your sister at the time?'

'My sister was eight.' He tore off a piece of flatbread and dipped it in a dark purple dip. 'My brother was sixteen.' He handed her the bread.

'You have a brother?'

'Rafa. He lives in England. The *baba ganoush* is good, yes?'

'Yes, it's delicious.' She licked a remnant of the dip from the corner of her mouth, frowning when she realised what he was doing. 'Why are you feeding me?'

His piercing gaze met hers. 'I like feeding you.'

Something happened to the air between them because suddenly Regan found it hard to draw breath. She reached for her water glass. Their conversation had taken on a deeply personal nature and it was extremely disconcerting.

'I can't stay here,' she husked. For one thing,

she needed to find Chad, and for another…for another, this man affected her on levels she didn't even know she had and she had no idea what to do about it.

'You have no proof that my brother did anything wrong.'

His gaze became shuttered. 'That topic of conversation is now closed.'

Agitated, Regan stared at him. 'Not until you tell me what makes you so certain Chad has taken your sister.'

Leaning back in his chair, he took so long to answer her she didn't think that he would. 'We have CCTV footage of them together and after she'd gone my sister left a message on my voicemail informing me that she was with a friend.'

Regan frowned. 'That hardly sounds like someone who has been taken against her will.'

'Milena is due to marry a very important man next month. She would not have put all of that at stake if she wasn't forced to do so.'

'Maybe she doesn't want to marry him any more.'

A muscle jumped in the King's jaw. 'She agreed to the marriage and she would never shirk her duties. Ever.'

His sister might have agreed, Regan mused silently, but having to marry out of duty would make most women think twice. 'Does she love the important man she's going to marry?'

'Love is of no importance in a royal marriage agreement.'

'Okay.' Regan thought love was important in *any* marriage agreement. 'I'll take that as a no.'

'You can take it any way you want,' he ground out. 'Love is an emotional concept and does not belong in the merger of two great houses.'

'Merger? You make it sound like a business proposition.'

'That is as good a way of looking at it as any.'

'It's also harsh. What about affection? Mutual respect? What about *passion*?'

She had no idea where that last had come from—she'd meant to say *love*.

His gaze narrowed in on her mouth and a hot tide of colour stung her cheeks. 'Those things can come later. After the marriage is consummated.'

'That's provided you marry someone nice,' Regan pointed out. 'What if this important man is horrible to her?'

'The Crown Prince of Toran will not be horrible to my sister or he will have me to answer to.'

'That's all well and good in principle, but it doesn't mean your sister *wants* it. I mean, don't get me wrong, there isn't anything I wouldn't do for my family, but when it comes to marriage I'd like to choose my own husband. Most women would.'

'And what would you choose?' His voice was deep and mocking. 'Money? Power? Status?'

His questions made Regan feel sorry for him. Clearly he'd met some shallow women in his time, which went some way to explaining his attitude. 'That is such a cynical point of view,' she replied. 'But no, those things wouldn't make my top three.'

'Let me guess,' he said, a sneer in his voice. 'You want kindness, a sense of humour, and someone to want you just for you.'

Surprised that he'd hit the nail on the head, Regan was flummoxed when he started laughing.

'I don't see what's so funny,' she griped. 'That's what most women want.'

'That's what most women *say* they want,' he retorted with masculine derision. 'I've found that those things fall far short of the mark unless money and power are involved.'

'Then I'd say you've been dating women far

short of the mark. Maybe you need to raise your expectations.'

'When I marry, Miss James, it will not be for kindness, love or humour.'

'No,' Regan agreed, 'I'm sure there'll be nothing funny about it. Or loving.'

His lips tightened at her comment. 'I don't need love.'

'Everyone needs love. Believe me, I see the kids in my classroom who aren't properly loved and it's heartbreaking.'

'I agree that a parent should love a child,' he rasped, 'but it's irrelevant in a marriage.'

'I disagree. My parents were deeply in love until the day they died. My father was someone who showed genuine love and affection to all of us.'

'No wonder you have a fairy-tale view of relationships.'

Regan tilted her head, wondering where his *un-fairy-tale-like* view had come from. 'What about your parents? Were they happily married?'

'My parents' marriage was a merger.'

'Not a surprise, I suppose, given your attitude, but I didn't ask why they married, I asked if they were happy.'

One minute he was sitting opposite her and the next he was standing at the windows, staring out at the darkening sky. He took so long to respond to her question, and was so still, Regan would have assumed he'd gone to sleep if not for the fact that he was standing up. Just as she was wondering what she could say to break the tension in the room he turned back to her, a scowl darkening his face. 'Whether my parents were happy or not is unimportant. But actually they weren't. They rarely saw each other. My mother found that she didn't have the stamina to be a queen and spent most of her time in Paris or Geneva. My father was King. A job that leaves little time for anything else. He did what needed to be done. As my sister will. As my brother will, and as I will.'

His words painted a somewhat bleak picture of his early years.

'That sounds a bit cold. Maybe your sister wants something different. Maybe she and my brother are in love. Have you considered that?'

If the muscle jerking in his jaw was any indication, then yes, he had considered it. And not happily.

'You'd better hope not,' he growled.

'Why not? What if they're in love and want to

get married?' God, what if they were *already* married? This man would probably skewer Chad like a pig on a spit-roast. 'Would that be such a big deal at the end of the day?'

The look he gave her was dangerous. Dangerous and uncompromising. 'Milena is already betrothed,' he bit out softly. 'And that betrothal cannot be broken. It *will not* be broken.'

'Tell me,' she said, narrowing her eyes, 'are you concerned about your sister's welfare because she's your sister or because she might ruin your precious plans with this so-called Crown Prince?'

'Are you questioning my affection for my sister?' he asked with deadly softness.

'No. I'm saying that if it's true and she and Chad are in love, what can you do about it? I mean, it's not like you can punish my brother for falling in love with your sister. You might not think it's important but falling in love is surely not a crime. Even here.'

The smile he gave her didn't reach his eyes. 'You don't know my country very well at all, Miss James, do you?' He stalked towards her and leaned over her chair, caging her in with his hands on either armrest.

Regan's heart knocked against her chest so

loudly she thought he'd be able to hear it. She wasn't afraid of him, although perhaps if she had any sense she would be, because the look in his eyes could chill lava. 'I can have your brother executed for just looking at my sister.'

Regan drew in a shocked breath. 'You cannot.'

His mouth twisted into a grim smile. 'You have no idea what I'm capable of.' His eyes drifted over her face and down to her body. Regan's breath hitched inside her chest. He was so close, his scent filled her senses and started acting like solvent on her brain. She wanted to tell him that she didn't care what he was capable of but neither her brain nor her body seemed to be functioning on normal speed.

'But all that is irrelevant. If you and your brother are as close as you claim to be then he will come running soon.'

With that arrogant prediction he straightened away from her, giving her body enough respite that she could finally drag air into her lungs.

'Goodnight, Miss James. I hope you enjoyed your dinner.'

Discombobulated by his nearness and the vacuum left by his sudden departure, Regan jumped to her feet and went after him, grabbing hold of the sleeve of his robe. 'Hold on a minute.' She blinked a few times to clear her head. 'What do you mean by that? Why will my brother come running?'

'Because hopefully he's seen the photos I've had released of the two of us.'

'Photos?'

'Yes.' His blue eyes glittered down into hers. 'It seems you and I were photographed together in the hotel lobby. By now they should be splashed all over the European news networks with your name attached.'

'You're using me as bait,' she whispered on a rushed breath.

'I like to think of it as insurance.' His superior smile did little to ease her rising temper. 'When your brother finds out you're here I'm hoping those familial connections you spoke so movingly about will have him scurrying out of the woodwork.'

'Oh, you are t-truly awful,' she stammered furiously. 'Your sister has run away because you're mean and trying to marry her off to someone who is probably just as horrible as you, and you're going to scare my brother in the process.'

'Your brother will pay for his sins, Miss James,

and if you two are as close as you say you are he'll come running.'

Regan shook her head. 'I've never met a man as cold and heartless as you. Something you're no doubt very proud of.' She shoved her hands on her hips and stared him down. 'You can't keep me here like this. When I tell the American consulate what you've done you'll be an international pariah.'

The look he gave her was cold and deadly, not a shred of compassion on the stark planes of his beautiful face. 'Are you threatening me, Miss James? You do know it's a crime to threaten the King?'

Regan tossed her hair back from her face. 'It's no doubt a crime to hit him as well but if I had a baseball bat handy, Sheikh Hadrid, or King Jaeger, or whatever your title is, I'd use it.'

She saw his nostrils flare and she suddenly realised how close together they were standing. If she took another step forward they'd be plastered up against each other. She told herself to do the opposite and step back but once again her body and her brain were on divergent paths.

'The correct title is *Your Majesty*,' he said

softly. 'Unless we're in bed. Then you can call me Jaeger, or Jag.'

Oh, God, why had he said that?

And why was he looking at her as if he wanted to devour her? As if he wanted to kiss her as much as she wanted to kiss him?

This is stupid, Regan, she warned herself. *Step back. Step back before it's too late.*

But she didn't step back; instead she poked the bear. Quite literally, with her pointer finger. 'Like that will ever happen,' she threw at him. 'I hate you. The only time I would *ever* sleep with you is in your dreams.'

'Is that so?'

He grabbed hold of the finger she was using to jab him and brought it to his mouth. Regan's breath backed up in her lungs as he ran the tip of her finger back and forth across his lower lip. Heat raced through her, consuming every ounce of good sense she'd ever owned. 'Don't do that,' she begged, her voice husky.

He looked down at her, his blue eyes blazing. 'Don't fool yourself. You don't hate me, little America. Far from it.'

CHAPTER FOUR

THE FOLLOWING MORNING Regan was still incensed by the King's high-handedness. Clearly nothing was beyond him: imprisonment, trickery, *sexual domination.*

'Don't fool yourself. You don't hate me, little America. Far from it.'

She did hate him. Of course she did. He was autocratic...arrogant... He was... The memory of the way his warm breath had moistened the tip of her finger, hinting at the dark heat of his mouth, made her shiver. He was unbelievably sexy!

Not that she was thinking about that. Or her response. She liked men who saw themselves as equal with women. King Jaeger obviously saw himself as equal with no one. Not even the gods!

'I make the rules here,' she muttered under her breath, completely oblivious to the beautiful, sultry day outside. 'You'll do as I say.'

How could she find a man like that sexy? Stress. Lingering jet lag. Inconvenient chemistry.

If only he were a rational man you could reason with. But he wasn't. He had decided her brother was guilty, and appealing to reason wasn't going to work.

Which left her with no option but to get away, or at the very least get word to Chad that she was fine and that he needn't worry about her. As much as she wanted to find out what was going on with him, she couldn't bear it if he panicked and did something crazy. Such as put himself in King Jaeger's path.

She glanced around the high walls that surrounded the gardens. She had thought about scaling them but had almost immediately dismissed the idea. They were about twenty feet high and smoothly rendered. There wasn't a foothold anywhere. She had also tried brazening it out and simply walking out of the door on the first day but it was always locked. The only time it wasn't was when the maid was cleaning, as she was now, but on those occasions a security guard was stationed outside the door.

Regan knew because she had tried to sneak out the day before and been met with his implacable, blank stare. Maybe the King trained them personally.

Frustrated at how utterly helpless she felt, she strode back inside. Had the photo of her in the King's arms been released to the media yet? Probably. She hated the thought that Chad had seen it and was worried about her, but more, she hated the thought of what would happen once King Jaeger got hold of her brother.

Good God, what had her brother been thinking, running off with a princess? Was he personally involved with her? And could the King really have him executed? More importantly, would he? He definitely seemed ruthless enough to do it but something told her that he wasn't as bad as he made out. Closed, yes. Bad…no.

Regan fought back a wave of helpless frustration, absently watching the maid enter something into her tablet before picking up the feather duster again. Regan didn't know what she could possibly be dusting—the room was immaculate. The maid was young, no more than twenty, at a guess, and seemed sweet enough. Unfortunately she spoke limited English, totally clamming up that first day when Regan had informed her that she wasn't a guest of the King and needed to leave the palace as quickly as possible.

The girl had given her a confused, shy smile

and told her in broken English how wonderful the King was, at which point Regan knew she wouldn't be getting any help from her direction.

But if King Jaeger thought she would sit back while he planned her brother's demise he was very much mistaken. As soon as she was free she would contact the American Embassy and demand that they…that they…what? Put in place economic sanctions against Santara? Ban tourism to the smaller nation? Most likely Jaeger would laugh and shrug those impossibly broad shoulders with a care factor of zero.

Irritated, she watched as the maid returned to her trolley and retrieved a cloth and cleaning agent before heading into the bathroom, leaving the trolley behind. Wandering around the room like a caged tiger in need of exercise, Regan passed the trolley and abruptly stopped when she realised that the maid had not only left her trolley unattended, but she'd left the tablet on it as well.

Heart thumping, she glanced towards the bathroom, where she could hear the maid singing softly to herself, and grabbed the electronic device. Praying that it wasn't password-protected, she nearly gave a cry of relief when the screen lit up at her touch.

Ignoring her sweaty palms, she quickly connected to the internet and chewed on her lip as she thought about what to do next. Not having expected to get access to the web, she had no idea who to contact. The American Embassy? Did they have an emergency email on their website? But even if she contacted them they would have no way of telling Chad that she was fine. That she wasn't at the mercy of King Jaeger. Worse, they might not even believe her.

Thinking on her feet, she pulled up her social-media account and had a brainwave. Rushing over to a sun lounger, she quickly unbuttoned her shirt so that her bra looked like a bikini. With trembling fingers she angled the tablet, plastered a bright smile on her face and took a photo of herself with the pool in the background. Then she quickly captioned a message underneath.

Having fun chez King Jag. Hope you are too. The King is a wonderful host! ♥♥♥

She grinned as she added the three heart emojis. They were a fun joke between her and Chad that she had started when he had been an easily embarrassed teenager. It was something her mother would have taken great joy in doing to both of them.

Before she could reconsider her actions she hit 'post' and watched it come up on her home page. It wasn't much, and she had no guarantee that Chad would check the site, but it was a way they had kept up with each other's lives after he'd gone to university. With any luck he would check it before panicking about what the heck she was doing in the King's arms.

Spiked with adrenaline at having outsmarted His high-and-mighty Majesty, she was about to write Chad a private message when she heard a noise in the room. Not wanting to alert the maid to what she had done, Regan quickly closed down the page she was on and strolled back inside, the tablet behind her back.

The maid didn't even look her way and Regan only realised that her whole body was shaking after she quickly put the device back on the trolley. She exhaled a rushed breath and tried to calm her heartbeat. The tablet wasn't in the same place as where she'd found it, but with any luck the maid would think that she had moved it herself.

Glancing at Regan quizzically, the young girl

returned to the trolley and gave her a small smile as she wheeled it out of the room.

A shiver snaked its way down Regan's spine. She had managed to thwart the King. She only hoped he never found out. A small smile touched her lips. But, even if he did, it wasn't as if he could do anything about it. The man didn't control the world.

Jag pounded his opponent so hard the man's knees nearly buckled beneath him.

He should never have gone to her suite. Never have argued with her and certainly never have brought her fingers to his lips.

He swung hard again, grunting as his gloved fists connected with solid muscle.

From now on she would stay on one side of the palace and he would stay on the other.

His opponent groaned loudly. 'Either I'm in really poor form, or you're in extremely good form today, boss-man.' Zumar winced as he prodded the side of his jaw. 'If I'm lucky I might get out of this bout still standing.'

Jag rolled his aching shoulders and waited for Zumar to resume his fighting stance. Zumar was six feet six, built like an iron tank, and the head chef in the palace. He'd once been a black belt in karate and a kick-boxing champion before injury had forced him into another career as a street fighter. Many years ago Jag had assisted him in a five-against-one street brawl and given him a second chance. Zumar had studied as a chef, and could now run a Michelin-star establishment if he so chose. He didn't. Instead he'd made a life for himself in Santara and remained loyal to Jag. Loyal until they faced off in the ring during their regular training sessions.

'Stop complaining,' Jag growled. 'I can't help it if you're going soft on all those pastries you bake.'

'Soft, is it?' Zumar laughed. 'Bring it on, boss-man.'

Jag did…taking out his pent-up energy and frustration in the ring rather than on the woman currently occupying his garden suite.

He still couldn't believe how close he'd come to kissing her again last night. The woman did things to his equilibrium he didn't want to contemplate. Because, for a man who was used to being in the utmost control at all times, it was a sad indictment to admit that when he'd taken one look at her in those cut-off shorts he'd nearly forgotten his own name.

Then there was all her talk of love and happiness…as if they were goals that motivated his life!

What did motivate him was success, position, power. Providing for his country and his family. Making sure everything ran smoothly and that Santara would never be in an inferior political position with its neighbours—Berenia and Toran—again. And if that made him a—what had she called him?—a stubborn, autocratic, overbearing tyrant, then so be it.

Usually steady on his feet, he felt Zumar's fist connect with his right cheekbone. He staggered sideways and scowled at his chef's ecstatic expression.

'Lucky shot,' he growled.

'I'll take it, boss-man,' Zumar chortled, raising his fists again.

Jag feinted a right hook to his jaw and then did a kick-boxing manoeuvre that brought the other man down.

'You learn too fast,' Zumar complained. 'I'm calling time.'

'You can't,' Jag stated. 'I'm not finished.'

'You want to cook your own meal tonight, boss-man?'

Jag grunted, wrapping his gloved hand around Zumar's and hauling him to his feet. He glanced around the basement gymnasium many of his senior officers also used, to see if there was anyone else who would help him work off some steam.

Regan James might, his recalcitrant libido whispered, *though that would be a very different type of workout from this.*

Ignoring that unhelpful thought, he tried to catch the eye of a few of his army officers. Unfortunately Jag had never been known to employ idiots and every man in the room kept his gaze averted. It wasn't hard to sense that their leader wasn't quite himself right now.

'What's up with you anyways, boss-man?' Zumar asked, wiping the sweat from his brow with a sports towel. 'This big-deal summit tying you up in knots?'

'It's not the summit.'

'A woman, then.'

'A woman?' Jag gave him a baleful look, yanking his gloves off. 'Why would you say that?'

The Nigerian shrugged. 'When a man is as worked up as you are it usually means trouble of the female variety.' He gave Jag a knowing grin. 'But there is no escape, huh? The heart knows what the heart wants.'

The heart?

'What about your parents? Were they happily married?'

From out of nowhere, Regan's unexpected question from the night before dredged up unwelcome memories of his childhood. He still couldn't fathom how he had become embroiled in a conversation about his family with her. He never talked about his parents, not his father's death, nor his mother leaving them when they were young. It had happened, he'd dealt with both events and moved on, as was befitting for the as then future King of Santara.

And no, he hadn't mourned his father's death. He hadn't thought to. He had respected his father and always done his duty by him, but he hadn't really known the man, other than as his King. And as for his mother…she had never asked for Jag's love and never wanted him to give it.

His throat thickened. Regan James didn't know what she was talking about with her fairy-tale ideas about life. She'd never known duty or hardship. She had never… He frowned. Actually, she had known duty and hardship. And still she remained soft and open. Trusting that people behaved the way that they should. *Little fool.*

Yes, he would be on one side of the palace, she on the other. Because whenever he was around her she managed to twist logic and common sense into something unrecognisable. And really, why would he see her again? She was a means to an end. When that end came about they'd part company and never see each other again. And wasn't that a cause for celebration?

He gave Zumar a hearty slap on the back. 'Thanks, Chef.'

Zumar blinked. 'What for?'

'For helping me realise what was wrong.'

Zumar cracked his jaw. 'Next time I'd appreciate you working that out *before* we get into the ring, boss-man.'

Jag laughed. It felt good to be on solid ground again. Back in charge.

Last night…the chemistry between them, the way she made him question himself… Gone. Completely gone.

At least it was right up until Tarik burst into his dressing room thirty minutes later, his forehead pleated like an accordion.

Jag immediately stopped whistling. 'Milena?'

'No, no, I have no updates on Milena, Your Majesty.'

Jag let out a relieved breath, pulling on his trousers. 'Then it's something to do with the American. I can see the signs of frustration on your face. Don't let it bother you. I imagine she has that effect on everyone she meets.'

'Yes, sir, it is the American woman.'

'What has she done now? Tied her bed sheets together and scaled the palace wall? Planned out my demise in three easy steps? Whatever it is,' Jag assured him as he pulled a white shirt from its hanger, 'I'm not going to let it ruin my good mood.'

'She connected to the internet and uploaded a picture of herself at the palace.'

'Say what?' Jag nearly tore a new armhole in his shirt as he thrust his arm through it. 'Let me see.'

Tarik turned the tablet around so that the screen faced him. He scanned the photo that showed way too much of Regan's sexy cleavage in an ice-blue bra.

Jag knew five Santarian dialects and he swore

in all five of them. 'Isn't that the pool in the garden suite?' he bit out.

'Yes, sir. This is a social-media post from the palace.'

He went still. 'The palace is not on social media.'

'No, sir, but Miss James is.'

'Miss James does not have a phone or any other device with her.'

'No. But she somehow got access to one and two hours ago she uploaded this post.'

'She got access to one?' Jag repeated softly. 'How?'

'The IT department is working on obtaining that information. They should know very soon.' There was a touch of desperation in Tarik's voice and Jag knew that his aide was trying to handle him.

'Take it down before anyone sees it,' he ground out. Like her brother, whom he had no doubt had been the troublesome woman's intended audience.

'I already ordered it to be taken down, Your Majesty.' Tarik swallowed heavily. 'Unfortunately it has already been seen.'

Jag paused in the process of buttoning his shirt,

a sense of foreboding turning his powerful frame tense. 'By whom?'

'The post has been shared across various multimedia outlets six million times, sir.'

'Six mill…' Jag scowled. 'How is that possible in so short a time frame?'

'You are a very popular monarch, Your Majesty, especially since the world is expecting you to announce your betrothal to Princess Alexa this weekend. And, with all eyes on Santara at present because of the impending summit, I'm surprised it's not more.'

Jaeger cursed viciously. He had completely forgotten about Princess Alexa.

'Quite,' Tarik agreed. 'But, speaking of your prospective engagement, I have King Ronan on the phone. He is furious that it seems you are entertaining a *concubine*—his words, sir—after agreeing to marry his daughter. He is threatening to call off the engagement and boycott the summit.'

Jag stared at Tarik. For the first time in his life his brain was struggling to keep up with the turn of events. As beautiful as Princess Alexa was, Jag had no real desire to marry her other than the convenience of it. She understood his world and, from what he knew of her, she was as logical and pragmatic as he was. She was also polished and poised. Any leader would be fortunate to have her on his arm. Not only that, but marrying her would strengthen ties with Berenia, Santara's third neighbour.

'Miss James is *not* my live-in mistress,' he bit out. 'And I have *not* formally agreed to marry Princess Alexa.'

'I know, Your Majesty, but King Ronan is clearly of the impression that you have.'

'That's because King Ronan is a pushy bastard who tries to manipulate people.'

'Of course, sir. But it is important that you have a plus-one this weekend. If King Ronan is not pacified he will not allow Princess Alexa to attend as your escort. And you know it is never a good idea to attend these events alone.'

Yes, he did, but he had more pressing matters to consider right now than a plus-one. He dragged a hand through his still damp hair. By rights he should be furious with Regan for this stunt—and he was—but part of him couldn't fault her ingenuity. Hell, he might even admire it if she wasn't causing him so much grief in the process.

'King Ronan is holding for you, Your Majesty. He wants to speak with you personally.'

'Of course he does.' Jag snatched up his cell phone from his dresser. 'Transfer the call to my personal number,' he ordered, his brain having gone from sluggish to full-on alert as he went into automatic problem-solving mode.

'Yes, sir.' Tarik flicked his finger quickly across the screen on his tablet. 'And Miss James?'

Jag scowled. 'Leave Miss James to me.' He'd strangle her as soon as he placated the volatile King of Berenia and made a decision about whether or not to marry the Princess.

Striding down the marble staircase en route to the garden suite, he brought his phone to his ear. 'King Ronan,' he said smoothly. 'I believe we have a small problem.'

CHAPTER FIVE

'COME ON, JUST sit still,' Regan crooned. 'Please, just for another few seconds.'

Her camera shutter clicked as she photographed a pair of olive and yellow birds with elegantly turned-down beaks. It was clear by the way they danced around each other and rubbed their beaks together that they were a couple, and their antics made her smile. They reminded her of humming-birds back home, and she'd always had a soft spot for photographing couples—both animal and human. Everyone loved the notion of finding their soulmate, and she found that 'couples' sold well as stock photos.

She checked her viewfinder, satisfied that the pretty pair would be very popular when they were uploaded onto her website. The light was magnificent in Santara, making the exotic colours of this timeless land pop. Just looking at the sweeping sands of the desert beyond the palace made her itch to explore it.

As concentrated as she was on capturing a shimmering mauve dragonfly hovering above the azure-blue of the pool with her lens, there was no mistaking the moment the King stormed into her suite. She heard the heavy door to her room bang forcefully against the wall, and turned to see a small cloud of white powder float to the floor from where the ornate handle had gouged the plaster.

Regan moved to the arched doorway and then blinked. King Jaeger stood inside her room, dressed in a pair of tailored trousers that hugged his powerful legs, an unbuttoned pristine white shirt, and that was it. His legs were braced wide, his hands held loosely at his sides, and he wore an expression on his face that could level a mountain. Regan couldn't prevent her eyes from running down the darkly tanned strip of flesh from his neck to the trousers that sat low on his hips. Dark hair covered his leanly muscled chest, arrowing down to bisect abdominal muscles you could probably bounce a coin off.

Her mouth ran dry as her gaze continued on down to his feet.

'I think you forgot your shoes,' she said, appalled to find that she even found the sight of his bare feet sexy.

The door closed behind him with a thud.

'And possibly your sense of humour,' she added, trying to lighten the mood and stop herself from obsessing about his body.

'If I were you I'd be very worried right about now,' he drawled menacingly.

She was. Worried that she couldn't stop thinking about sex whenever he was around. It was becoming insidious.

'About?' she asked, deciding to brave out his obviously bad mood. It wasn't possible that he'd found out about her post so quickly. Not unless he had ESP, or security cameras in her room. She cast a quick glance at the corners of the ceilings. Nothing there. Thank heavens.

'How did you do it?' he asked softly.

Damn. He did know. 'Do what?'

'Don't play cute with me—it won't work. How did you access the internet?'

'Oh, that…' She strolled further into the room until she'd put the protection of the sofa between them. He didn't have the look of a man who was about to do her physical harm, and indeed, every time he had restrained her she'd felt him leash his physical strength so as not to hurt her, but she suspected that if his temper ever did blow it would make Mount Vesuvius look as innocuous as a child throwing sand.

'Yes. *That.*' He came towards her, with animal grace, the muscles in his abdomen rippling with every silent footfall. Regan swallowed, her own stomach muscles pulling tight at the sight. A rush of excitement shot through her. *Excitement?* Was she completely daft? The man looked as if he was coming up with new ways she was going to die!

He stopped in front of the sofa, his eyes briefly scanning it before returning to her. It wouldn't be enough, she thought wildly; the Great Wall of China wouldn't be enough to keep her from him if he wanted to get to her.

'So I accessed the internet,' she murmured vaguely. 'I didn't write anything negative. I actually implied that I liked you. Which I don't, in case you get any ideas.'

Or, at least, any more ideas...

'You implied a lot more than that,' he muttered furiously.

'You're just unhappy because I countered your move and foiled your horrible plan to worry Chad. How did you find out so quickly, by the way? Do you have cameras in this room, watching my every move? That would be truly creepy if you did.'

'I do not have cameras in here, though I might after this,' he bit out. 'But, in answer to your question, your post has been shared a number of times.'

'Good,' she said. 'I hope Chad has managed to see it.'

'I know Chad was your intended audience.' His thick dark lashes narrowed, making his blue eyes seem impossibly vibrant. 'Unfortunately you picked up a few more *interested* parties.'

Regan frowned at his deceptively light tone. 'How many more?'

'Six million more.'

'Six mill—! That can't be true. I only have forty-eight followers and most of those are work-related.'

'You might not be popular, Miss James, but I am.'

'Lucky you,' she retorted, wishing he'd worn more clothing. 'Don't you want to button your shirt?' she said, inwardly cringing at the husky note in her voice when she'd been aiming for cool. 'It's quite chilly today.'

'It's forty degrees in the shade. And I'll button my shirt when I'm good and ready.' His voice became a lethal purr. 'Unless it's bothering you...'

'No. Not at all.' She waved off his suggestion as if it were ludicrous. 'I was just thinking that it didn't look very...*kingly*.'

His smile said that he knew she was lying. 'Good, because I'm not feeling very *kingly* right now.' His eyes drifted to her lips and Regan barely resisted the urge to moisten them. Sexual tension arced between them like a tightrope, and she had no idea what to do with all the jittery energy that coursed through her. She felt like a small child in a room full of sweets who had been told to stand in the corner and not touch anything.

Heat suffused her cheeks and she tried not to think about how warm and resilient his skin would feel if she were to slide her hands inside his open shirt. 'Of course, how you walk around the palace is entirely up to you. Don't mind me.'

She bit into her lip to stop the nervous chatter. She hoped the sharp little pain would also stop all the inappropriate thoughts running through her head.

'Thanks for the memo,' he bit out tautly. 'Now stop prevaricating and tell me how you did it.'

'I can't.' One thing she wouldn't do was get the lovely girl who cleaned her room into trouble.

A muscle ticked in his jaw. 'Miss James, I am two seconds away from strangling you with my bare hands and feeding your body to a lake full of alligators. I suggest you don't push me any further.'

'There are alligators in the desert?'

'Regan!'

She jumped as he bellowed her name. He'd never used her first name before and it scattered her thoughts. 'Calm down.' She didn't know if she was referring to him or herself, but it didn't matter. 'I was only asking. But...' She couldn't think of any more stalling tactics, so she just went with honesty. 'I have no intention of telling you how I accessed the internet, so stop asking me.'

'If someone in my employ helped you they will be punished.'

Regan planted her hands on her hips. 'It wasn't her fault.'

Jaeger's blue eyes narrowed, assessing. 'The maid helped you.'

'She didn't help me. She had a tablet and I... borrowed it.'

The muscle in his jaw flexed rigidly.

'If you punish her I'll never forgive you,' she said earnestly, 'because it wasn't her fault.'

'I have no doubt it wasn't her fault but it is obvious she was negligent.'

'I took advantage.'

'Believe me, I'm in no doubt about that.'

'So you won't do anything to her?' she implored. 'Because I can't allow it.'

'*You* can't allow it?'

He coughed out a laugh and Regan folded her arms across her chest. 'No. It wouldn't be fair. And you strike me as a very fair man.'

'Stop playing to my vanity.' He shook his head. 'It hasn't worked with women before you; it won't work for you either.'

'I was only—'

'Quiet,' he growled. 'I need to think.'

He might need to but she could really use some air.

'Where are you going?'

Regan looked over her shoulder to find him watching her. 'There's no need to shout,' she grouched. 'I'm right here. And you clearly don't need me to think.'

'I never shout,' he corrected her. 'At least, I didn't before I met you.'

Seriously unnerved by the effect his near naked body was having on her Regan's heart hammered inside her chest. 'You know how to fix that,' she said faintly. 'You can let me go.'

He laughed. 'I wish I could. Believe me, you're a nuisance I could well do without.'

For some reason his words hurt. For all the unconventional nature of their meeting, and their missing siblings, Regan couldn't deny that he was the most exciting man she had ever met. Since her parents had died she'd become cautious and responsible. She always played it safe. One look at this man, one touch, made her feel electrified and more alive than she'd felt in so long. The feeling was at once thrilling and completely appalling. The man didn't *do* love and that was all she knew how to do.

He let out a rough breath that brought her eyes back to his. 'You have no idea what you've done, do you?' he muttered.

Something in his tone stayed her. 'Should I?'

'No. I suppose not.' He dragged a hand through his hair, mussing it further. 'In your world, posting a provocative image on social media would barely raise a ripple. Here it is very different. Here we have morals and ethics.'

'We have morals and ethics in America,' Regan said a little defensively. Well, they used to, at least, and most still did.

'Be that as it may, what you have done, Miss James,' he said with palpable restraint, 'is create a diplomatic crisis I am now in a position to have to fix.'

'A diplomatic crisis? I don't see how.'

'I have probably the most important summit my country has ever hosted starting tomorrow and a raft of people wondering who the American woman is I'm entertaining in my palace.'

'You're hardly entertaining me.'

'Further, I am now without an escort for the next four days.'

'I fail to see what this has to do with me.'

'Then let me explain it to you.' His blue eyes glittered down into hers. 'Since you have created this issue, you will become the escort you made me lose.'

'I didn't make you lose anyone,' she denied hotly. 'And there's no way I'm going to be your escort.' She gave a shaky laugh. Just the thought of it made her hot. 'Do you know what people would think if they saw us together?'

His eyes turned smoky and he leant against the back of the sofa, one bare foot crossed over the other, his eyes on her denim shorts. 'I think that horse has already bolted, *habiba*.'

Regan swallowed heavily. 'Well, I don't intend to make it worse by being seen on your arm. And anyway, this is all really your fault for bringing me here in the first place.'

'I agree. But that horse has also bolted, and now we deal with the consequences.' His eyes turned hard. 'Usually Milena would step in during these situations, but we both know why she can't do that, don't we?'

Regan grimaced. 'My brother had nothing to do with your sister going AWOL! But okay,' she added quickly when she noticed the betraying muscle clench in his jaw. 'I think the best thing we can do now is leave things as they are. I won't cause any more problems,' she promised. 'And soon enough everyone will forget all about my little photo.'

'No one will forget you're here after that *little* photo. But even if they did, that doesn't solve all of my problems.'

'Surely you have women on speed dial all over the world who could play hostess—escort—for you. Probably any one of them would jump at the chance to do it.'

'I'm sure you're right.' His gaze travelled over her in blatant male appraisal. 'But the women I have on speed dial fulfil a very different function from hostessing, *habiba*.' His lazy drawl left her in no doubt as to what that function was. 'And I don't want to spend the weekend with a woman who might think that I'm more interested in her than I am. With you I know that won't happen.'

'Oh, you can count on that.'

A smile played around the edges of his mouth, amusement lighting his eyes. 'Why is it you're the only person who ever has the gumption to argue with me?'

'Probably if someone else had we wouldn't be in this dilemma because you'd have developed a sense of reason.'

'Oh, we'd be in it.'

'You might be,' she said irritably. 'But I wouldn't. I work at a prestigious private school. I have my reputation to think about, and once this is all over I'll be returning to my normal life and I'm not doing that as some hot desert king's mistress!'

'Hot?'

'As in temperature,' she said, her face flushing. 'You're like a furnace.' He laughed, which only irritated her more. 'Probably my friend, Penny, has already left me a tonne of messages on my phone asking me what's going on. Not that I'd know about those.'

'She has. My staff have replied on your behalf.'

'Oh…!' Her lips pressed into a flat line. 'I promised myself I wasn't going to let you make me angry again, but I'm struggling.'

'Good to know. And I understand your dilemma.'

'You do?'

'Yes. Which is why I won't present you as my partner, or escort. I'll present you as my fiancée.'

'Your *what*?'

Ignoring her shocked outburst, he paced back and forth. 'Yes, this is a much better solution. It will not only satisfy the curiosity of those wondering why you're in my palace, but, since the photo of you in my arms didn't bring your brother running to your rescue, news of our betrothal might do that job too.'

'You're as ruthless as a snake,' she spluttered. 'But it won't work. Chad would never believe it.'

'He doesn't have to believe it.' His bright blue eyes connected with hers. 'He just has to bring my sister back unharmed.'

Regan frowned. If Chad knew she was engaged to the King there was no doubt he'd come running. And maybe that was for the best. Then this whole situation would be resolved and she could go home. 'And if it doesn't work?'

'It has to work.'

'Why? Because your mightiness has decreed that it will?'

He stopped pacing to stare at her. 'You like challenging me, don't you, Regan?' His gaze lingered on her lips and her pulse jumped erratically in her throat.

'Yes, you should look wary,' he murmured. 'Right now I want to put my hands on you and I'm not sure if I want to make it pleasurable or painful.'

Regan jumped away from him, her insides jittery. 'We were talking about my brother,' she reminded him huskily.

'The whole reason you're here.'

He slowly prowled towards her, crowding her to the point where all she could think about was him. How tall he was. How big. How the stubble on his jaw would feel beneath her fingertips.

'Stop thinking of our betrothal in the romantic sense,' he advised. 'It's a business arrangement and it's temporary.'

'Two things you're obviously exceptionally good at.'

His jaw hardened and his gaze dropped to her mouth. 'I'm good at a lot of things, Regan, and if you're not careful you'll find out which of those things I'm *particularly* good at.'

Regan's mouth went dry at the sensual threat and once more she was acutely aware that he *still hadn't buttoned his shirt.*

He shook his head. 'Your desperation not to marry me serves you well, but it only reinforces that this is the right thing to do. My personal aide has been insisting for years that I need a partner at these major events, and having you by my side will mitigate any potential fallout from your ill-timed photo—'

'*My* ill-timed photo?'

'—And stop any untoward gossip from developing about the Western woman residing in my palace.'

'Residing?' She huffed out an astonished breath. 'You mean imprisoned.'

'If you were imprisoned you'd be in jail.'

'But this is all one-way. This is all about you and what you want. But what about what I want?'

'You're not in any position to make demands.'

'Actually, I am.' She threw back her head and stared at him. 'If you want my co-operation this weekend then I want something too.'

His body went preternaturally still and Regan got the distinct impression he thought she was going to ask him for money or jewels or something. 'You must have really dated some shallow women if the look of dread that just crossed your face is anything to go by.'

His eyes flashed blue sparks at her. 'Don't keep me waiting, Miss James; what is it you want?'

'A deal.'

'Excuse me?'

'Since deals are the only thing you seem to understand, I'll make one with you. I'll agree to be your escort, or rather, your partner this weekend if you let Chad go when he returns.'

'Absolutely not.' He swung away from her and then back. 'Your brother has my sister. That will not go unpunished.'

'But you don't really know what's happened or why they're together.'

'I will. And when I do your brother will be in serious trouble.'

'Fine; then you'll have to pull out your little black book and explain why you've locked me up some other way.'

He stalked over to the window and dug his hands into his pockets. Regan did her best not to notice the way the fabric of his trousers pulled tight across his well-defined glutes.

They're just muscles, she told herself, *just like the ones in his arms, his chest, his thighs...*

'Deal.'

What?

Her head came up, a betraying blush burning her face when she realised he had caught her staring.

'I'm agreeing with you. You become my fiancée for three nights and four days and when your brother returns, as long as my sister is unharmed, I'll let him leave the country. Unharmed.' He prowled towards her and she unconsciously backed up a step at the light of battle in his eyes. 'Rest assured, though.' He stopped just short of touching her. 'If my sister is hurt in any way I'll kill him, are we clear?'

'Rest assured,' Regan fired back at him. 'If my brother has caused your sister harm in any way you won't have to kill him—I will. But he won't have,' she added softly. 'Chad isn't like that. He's not a macho kind of guy who takes what he wants. He's kind and considerate.'

'Unlike me?' he suggested silkily.

'I didn't say that.'

'You didn't have to, *habiba*; your face is very expressive.'

God, she hoped not.

'Like for the last half hour,' he murmured, taking another step towards her, 'you've been wondering what it would be like to kiss me.'

Regan sputtered out some unintelligible noise that might have had the words 'massive' and 'ego' in it, her hands coming up between them to press firmly against his hard, *naked* chest. She bit her lip against the urge to slide them up that warm wall of muscle and twine them together at the nape of his neck. 'You're wrong,' she husked.

A light came into his eyes that turned her lips as dry as his dusty desert land. 'I'm not wrong.

Your pupils are dilated and your pulse is hammering, begging for me to put my mouth on it.'

His words caused hot colour to surge into her face. 'That's fear.'

His eyes lifted to hers. 'Fear of what?' he asked softly. 'That I will kiss you, or that I won't?'

Regan started to shake her head, a soft cry escaping her lips when his hands threaded into her hair and framed her face. His gaze held hers for an interminable second and then something coalesced behind his blue eyes and his head lowered to hers.

Regan's body jerked against his, her hands gripping his wrists with the intention of dragging them away from her, but it didn't happen. His mouth moved on hers with such heat and skill she went still beneath the onslaught. He gave a husky groan as his tongue traced the line between her lips, urging them to part. Sensation rocked through her and without any conscious thought her lips were shaping themselves to his, her mouth matching his hungry intensity.

With consummate skill, he completely controlled the kiss, one of his hands tunnelling further into her hair, angling her head so he could deepen the contact, the other pressed to the small of her back, urging her lower body to fit against his.

At the feel of his rock-hard desire, Regan moaned, wrapping her arms around his shoulders, her senses spinning out of control as she moved against him, her neck arching for the glide of his lips and tongue scraping against her skin.

He made a growling noise in the back of his throat that she felt deep in her pelvis, making her ache.

'Regan, I...' His lips returned to hers, his tongue exploring her mouth with a carnal intimacy that shocked her, the kiss going from hot to incendiary within seconds.

Regan heard herself moan, felt awash with sensations she couldn't contain. Her breasts were heavy and aching, desperate for relief, and her pelvis felt hollow. Beyond thought or reason her hands kneaded his shoulders, her fingers pushing aside his shirt to stroke his heated flesh.

He vibrated against the contact and his own hands must have moved, because suddenly he was cupping her breast, his thumb strumming the hard nub of her nipple, drawing a keening sound from deep inside her. She felt the need in him ramp up, his movements hungrier, more urgent as his hands skimmed over her body, his fingers tugging on her blouse to release the row of buttons, revealing the upper swell of her breasts to his lips and teeth.

Regan's hands gripped fistfuls of his hair, urging him closer. 'Jaeger... Jag. Please...' His name on her lips seemed to shift something in both of them. He lifted his mouth from her body, his breathing hard, his eyes almost black.

She sucked in a breath, tried to clear her head. She saw shock register on his face and knew instantly that he regretted what had just happened.

'Why did you do that?' She touched her fingers to her tender lips, swollen from the force of his kisses.

His eyes narrowed on her, somehow a lot clearer than hers. 'I've wanted to taste you since the first moment I met you. Now I have.' He stepped further away from her, his eyes mirroring the mental distance he was placing between them as well as the physical. 'Tomorrow you will be provided with a wardrobe that should cover everything you need for the next four days. As long as you stick to your side of the agreement, I'll stick to mine.'

With that he pivoted on his feet and walked out of the door.

As soon as it clicked closed Regan let out a pent-up breath and pressed her hand to her abdomen.

'I've wanted to taste you since the first moment I met you. Now I have.'

Her hand trembled as she pushed her hair back from her face.

Was he serious?

How could he kiss her like that and then walk away? How was that possible when she felt as if her world had been tipped upside down and shaken loose?

Well, because he must have kissed a thousand women to the half a dozen men she had kissed, most of which had occurred in high school before her parents had died. She'd never been great with boys and as she'd matured she hadn't been great with men either. The ones who liked her she had zero interest in, and the ones she thought had potential were not interested in a woman raising a teenage boy. Even if that boy was her brother. No way had anyone ever kissed her with the sensual expertise she'd just experienced with King Jaeger. But maybe kings were good at everything. Jag certainly claimed to know everything.

She shook her head, pride fortifying her spine. If he could walk away from that kiss without a backward glance then so could she.

Unconsciously her fingers went to her mouth and stroked down the side of her neck along the same path his lips had taken. When she realised what she was doing she dropped her hand and picked up her camera.

Reliving whatever it was that had just happened between them was not conducive to forgetting it. And forgetting it was exactly what she needed to do. She wasn't here for him. She was here for Chad. And now a deal she'd made on the fly.

A deal with the devil.

A deal she knew she could *never* go through with.

CHAPTER SIX

JAG KNEW AS soon as he spotted her in the small anteroom beside the grand ballroom that she was going to renege on their deal. And really he should let her. He didn't really give a damn about having a plus-one for the weekend. He'd done hundreds of these events before on his own. What would one more matter? And as to her unexplained presence in the palace...that was tougher to handle, but not impossible.

He paused for a moment, just watching her. She was pacing back and forth, her teeth delicately worrying her lower lip. A lower lip he had taken gently between his teeth not twenty-four hours earlier.

She looked astonishingly beautiful dressed in a slender column of burnished copper silk overlaid with a sheer organza bodice that accentuated the long line of her neck and hinted at the delicate swell of her breasts. The colour perfectly matched her hair, as he'd known it would, and turned her skin to polished ivory. Skin that was as soft as it looked.

Regan paused in front of the ornate mirror above the fireplace, tucking a strand of hair back behind her ear. Their gazes met in the mirror, her wide cinnamon eyes bright and lovely, her luscious lips painted a subtle pink. With her hair piled on top of her head in an elaborate style, she looked like an ethereal queen from a bygone era, and in that moment he knew he couldn't release her from their deal. Not yet.

Unwilling to analyse his motivations for that decision too closely, he leaned against the doorjamb. 'It's too late to change your mind, *jamila*,' he said gruffly.

She turned towards him with a suddenness that made the skirt of her gown swirl around her body, outlining her long legs before resettling. 'How do you know I want to change my mind?' she asked, her eyes gliding down over his body as if she couldn't help herself. He knew the feeling.

'Body language.'

He only hoped she wasn't as good at reading it as he was. If she was she'd know his was shouting, *I want you. Now.*

Uneasy at the depth of his primal response to her, he reminded himself that he'd already had this discussion with himself in the shower and it wasn't going to happen. He was not going to touch her again, or kiss her, and if that was all he could think about, well, that was just too bad. He wouldn't allow himself to complicate an already complicated situation. It wasn't logical. Just as kissing her hadn't been. One minute he'd been staring into her beautiful, expressive eyes and the next his hands were in her hair and his lips were soldered to hers.

She was like a magnet, and in that moment he'd had all the willpower of a metal shaving. It wasn't something he liked to acknowledge, even to himself.

Pushing away from the door, he strolled into the room. 'We have a few housekeeping issues to sort out before we—'

'Your Majesty, wait. Please.' She drifted closer and his nostrils flared as he picked up her delicate jasmine scent. He'd made sure that she'd been kept busy all day with spa treatments and massages, and just the thought of how supple her scented body would be was a sweet torture he could well do without.

'It's Jaeger,' he reminded her. 'Or Jag. Remember?'

She blushed a becoming shade of pink and pursed her lips. 'I'm trying not to.'

'Look, if this is about that kiss yesterday—'

'It's not about the kiss,' she cut him off quickly. 'I know what that was. You've already said. You wanted to know what it would be like to kiss me, you found out, and now you don't want to repeat the experience. We can move on from that.'

Move on? He wasn't sure that he could.

'The fact is, there's no way I can pose as your fiancée. I'm not royal, or a supermodel. I'm an ordinary schoolteacher. Everyone will know instantly that I'm a fraud.'

'You're not ordinary and I don't want you to pretend to be anyone but yourself. As a teacher you must be used to standing in front of large groups of people. I'm sure this won't be any different.'

He paced away from her, his mind still spinning at what she'd just said to him. Should he correct her misconception that he didn't want to repeat their kiss, or would it be easier to let it stand?

Unable to form a decision about that on the spot, he shelved it for later.

'I'm used to standing up in front of primary-school children,' she explained, 'which is not the same as what will be expected of me this week-end. And honestly, I'm a better behind-the-scenes person. I don't do well when the focus is directly on me. I get nervous.'

'Why?' Jag had dealt with crowds and atten-tion his whole life. He was so used to being scru-tinised from afar he didn't even give it a second thought. It was being scrutinised from up close that made him uncomfortable.

'I think it stems from all the impromptu inter-views from the child-protection services I had to undergo in the early years. Whenever I was under the spotlight there was always the chance that Chad would be taken away from me. I never wanted to let him down by not being good enough and as a result I really dislike surprises and I es-pecially dislike being the centre of attention.'

Shocked that she would tell him something so deeply personal, Jag felt something grip tight in his chest. 'I promise you that you won't be the centre of attention.' He reached out to stroke the side of her face and thought better of it. 'Don't forget, this is a political summit, not a day at Royal Ascot. That means I'll be the one in demand.' He kept his voice deliberately light, wanting to put her at ease and erase the vulnerability he saw in her expression. Vulnerability led to pain and the last thing he wanted was for her to suffer because of him. 'Now, the first part of housekeeping...' he reached into his pocket and pulled out a matte red box '...is for you to wear this.' He opened the box and turned it towards her.

'Oh, my God. It's as big as an iceberg,' she said, snatching her hands behind her back. 'I can't wear that.'

Jag smiled at her response. 'It was the biggest one I could find. Give me your hand.'

'No.'

Ignoring her small act of rebellion, he gently took hold of her left forearm and dragged her hand out from behind her back. 'I hope it fits. I had to guess the size of your fingers. They're so slender the jeweller thought I'd made a mistake.'

They both stared down at the intricately cut diamond glowing on her finger as if it had its own light source. 'But of course you didn't,' she said huskily. 'Are you sure it's not loaded with some beacon so you always know where I am?'

'Don't give me any ideas, *jamila*.'

She blinked up at him. 'You called me that before. What does it mean?'

'Beautiful.'

'I'm not—'

'Yes, you are.'

Awareness throbbed between them and Jag fought with the need to drag her into his arms and ruin her pink lipstick.

'Your Maj—'

'Jag,' he growled.

'This is too much,' she said thickly, keeping her eyes averted from his. 'I hope it's not real. I'll be afraid someone will rob me.'

'Nobody is going to rob you. Not in this crowd, but if it makes you feel any better my security detail will not let you out of their sights.'

'Are you sure that's not so I won't run off with it myself?'

'You won't run off with it. If you did I'd catch you. And yes, it is real.'

She pressed her lips together, staring at the

ring, and he had to curb another powerful need to soften the strain around her mouth with a kiss.

'There are three other items of housekeeping to go through,' he said briskly. 'Protocol demands that you always walk two paces behind me, and you also cannot touch me.' He noticed her tapered brows rise with astonishment, and he nodded. 'Santarians do not go in for PDAs.'

'Not ever?'

'Sometimes with children. If the family is a tactile one.'

'Wow, my parents would have been locked up, then. They were always hanging all over each other. And us. Chad and I definitely inherited their affectionate nature. Oh…' She gave him a disconcerted look. 'You probably didn't want to hear that.'

No, he hadn't. But more because he couldn't stop thinking about how wild she'd been in his arms the night before. And of course he didn't want to entertain the idea that Milena was having a relationship with Chad. *She wouldn't be strong enough to cope if it turned bad.* 'The third item is that I do not intend to spend the evening talking about your brother or my sister. It is a topic that is off the table from this moment on. Understood?'

'Perfectly. And I agree. It wouldn't look good if we started arguing in front of your guests.'

'My lords, ladies and gentlemen, *mesdames et messieurs*, I give you Sheikh Jaeger al-Hadrid, our lord and King of Santara, and his intended, the future Queen of Santara, Miss Regan James.'

Regan gave a small gasp at the formal introduction. She stood two steps behind Jag, waiting for him to descend the grand staircase, craning her neck to see over his wide shoulders to the room below. What she could see took her breath away. The room looked like a golden cloud, the walls gilt-edged and inlaid with dark turquoise wallpaper. Ancient frescoes and golden bell-shaped chandeliers adorned the high ceilings, while circular tables, elegantly laid with silverware and crystal, filled the floor space. Beautifully dressed men and women, some in military garb and traditional robes, milled in small groups and stared up at them with eager, over-bright eyes. Some, mostly the women, were craning their own necks to get a look at her, and it made Regan shrink back just a little more in the shadows.

When Jag had first informed her that she would have to walk two steps behind him at all times she'd been offended. Now she wondered if that wasn't a blessing. It might mean that she went unnoticed the whole night!

She twisted the egg-sized diamond on her finger, eyeing the endless row of steps they needed to descend with mounting dread. She just hoped she didn't trip over the beautiful gown she'd been squeezed into. It was the most delicate, the most exquisite piece of clothing she had ever worn and it made her feel like a fairy princess.

Queen, she amended with a grimace. Had Tarik really needed to introduce her as the future Queen? Couldn't he have just said her name? Or, better yet, nothing at all?

She noticed Jag shift in front of her and her heartbeat quickened. *Here we go*, she thought, preparing to follow him down the staircase. Only that didn't happen. As if sensing her unease, he turned towards her, his hand outstretched.

Regan glanced up to find sapphire-blue eyes trained on her with an intensity that made her burn. And just like that she was back in his arms with his mouth open over hers. She moistened her lips and saw his eyes darken in response. His chest rose and fell as he took a couple of deep breaths and she wondered if he wasn't thinking about the same thing. Then he gestured for her to approach him.

She took a small step, then another. 'What?' she whispered self-consciously. 'Why have we stopped?'

'The thing is…' A wry grin curled one side of his mouth and he looked so impossibly handsome in that moment she could have stared at him forever. 'The thing is, I've always hated protocol.' He drew her to his side and clasped her hand.

A low murmur rippled through the crowd as he raised her hand to his lips, a sexy smile lighting his eyes. It was a chivalrous gesture. A gesture meant to impress, and it did, melting Regan's heart right along with every other woman's in the ballroom.

Do not get caught up in all this, she warned herself, instantly suppressing the shiver of emotion that welled up inside her. This was not a fairy-tale situation. She was not Cinderella, and Jag was not going to be the Prince—or King— who promised to adore her for ever. Real life didn't work out that way. Real life was often a painful slog.

She gave him a faltering smile, wondering why he was still stalling. 'It's too late to change your mind now,' she whispered, throwing his earlier words back at him.

His smile widened. 'I have no intention of changing my mind, my little America.'

Regan told herself not to get lost in that smile. Or the nickname that sounded too much like an endearment. He had walked away from their kiss last night without a backward glance. The only interest he had in her was with regard to thwarting diplomatic crises and getting his sister back. That settled in her mind, she took a deep breath and concentrated on not tripping.

Unbelievably the night went much faster than Regan had expected. The people she met were mostly lovely and interesting, and Jag never let her very far out of his sight, instinctively sensing when she was feeling out of her depth and coming to her side.

'He's divine,' more than one woman had said with unabashed envy throughout the night, giggling like schoolgirls when Jag paid them personal attention. She watched with fascination at how he skilfully worked the room and put the people around him at ease. It was such a contrast to the way they had met, and yet she saw both elements of him in the superbly tailored tuxedo that did wicked things to his body. He was at once incredibly sophisticated and also inherently dangerous. Not physically. At least not to her. No, King Jaeger's danger was in the masculine charisma he exuded with unassailable ease. It made everyone in the room want to be near him. Especially her.

Realising that the wife of a Spanish diplomat had just spoken to her, Regan smiled apologetically. She cast a sideways glance at Jaeger, watching the way he easily commanded the conversation in the small group of delegates clustered around him. A stunning woman at his side leaned close to him and whispered something in his ear, her hand placing something into his trouser pocket so effortlessly Regan nearly missed it.

'You are very lucky,' the woman, Esmeralda, said again, forcing Regan to refocus.

'Lucky?' Regan murmured, wondering what they were talking about now.

'Yes. He is a king amongst kings.' She gave Regan a knowing smile. 'Although I'm not sure I could handle all that latent sexuality, and I'm Latin.'

Regan's face flamed as she recalled the sexual skill with which he'd kissed her, the way his hands had moulded her to him and stroked her breasts.

'Ooh-la-la...' Esmeralda chortled. 'I can see that you can.'

'Can what?' Jag asked smoothly, placing his arm around Regan's waist.

'Just girl talk, Your Majesty,' the older woman said, raking her eyes over his torso as if she wished it were her blood-red fingernails instead.

But Regan was embarrassed, knowing for a fact that the woman's assumptions were completely wrong. She didn't have the experience, or the expertise, to handle someone of Jaeger's sexual nature and she never would.

Excusing them both, Jag led her towards their table.

'What's in your pocket?' Regan asked, leaning close to him so no one could overhear.

He stopped and looked at her, stepping to the side to avoid anyone else following in their path. His eyes glinted with amusement at her. 'I suspect it's a phone number. I haven't looked.'

Regan's mouth fell open. She wasn't sure what astonished her the most. That he hadn't looked or that a woman would slip a man her phone number in plain sight of anyone who happened to be paying attention.

'But you're engaged,' she said on a rush. 'At least, that woman thinks you are.'

'She's also married.' His eyes twinkled as they gazed into hers.

'That's terrible. I don't know who to feel sorry for more—her or her husband. She's clearly not happy in her marriage.'

'Some people just want the excitement of being with someone new.'

'Well, I wouldn't. If I committed to someone I'd always be faithful to them.'

'As would I, *habiba*.' His voice was rough, as if he were speaking directly to her and not in generalities.

Her heart bumped inside her chest. 'So you do have scruples,' she said huskily.

'Just because I don't let anyone mess with my family, that doesn't make me the bad guy you think I am, Regan.'

He settled his hands on her waist and Regan's pulse leapt in her throat. 'I didn't think Santarians were into public displays of affection,' she murmured breathlessly.

'We're not,' he confirmed, leading her back

towards their table. 'But I figured I'd already broken protocol once tonight and the sky didn't fall in.'

She shook her head. 'You're a real rebel, aren't you?'

He laughed softly. 'Actually I'm not. I was always the child who did the right thing and toed the line growing up.'

'The dutiful son. Was that because it was expected of you as the first born?'

'That and because it was the only thing that made sense.'

'Love makes sense,' she said softly.

'For you, not for me.'

'Why do you think that?'

'Because I know how the world works. Both my parents were emotional. Their relationship unbearably volatile. Whenever emotion took over my mother left and my father worked harder. If there's one thing I've learned from watching my parents it's never to let emotion get in the way of making decisions.'

'But how do you control that so well?'

Right now all she could think about was wrapping her arms around his neck and dragging his mouth down to hers. It was actually frightening, the amount of times she thought about touching him. It felt as if she'd been in a deep sleep for a long time, only to waken and imprint on him like a baby bird.

'Practice.' He smiled at her, his teeth impossibly white against the dark stubble that had already started shading his jaw, taking him from merely handsome to outrageously gorgeous.

'Okay, well, I'm going to start practising emotionlessness right now. If you'll excuse me, I'm going to freshen up.'

'Don't be long.'

Regan let out a ragged breath as his gaze held hers. For a split second his eyes had been on her mouth and she could have sworn they had turned hungry. Most likely wishful thinking on her part.

She really didn't want to like him after the way he had threatened her brother and detained her as bait, but she knew that she did. Maybe if he hadn't kissed her she'd feel differently. But that wasn't entirely true. She'd found herself drawn to him even before she knew he kissed like a god. But he wasn't the only one who tried not to let their emotions dominate their decisions. She'd had to put her own aside after her parents died.

And worse, she knew no one was indispensable, so why put yourself out there in the first place?

'Excuse me.'

'Oh, I'm sorry.' Regan smiled at a beautiful dark-haired woman as she exited the ladies' room. She stepped to the side so the woman could enter but she shook her head.

'I'm not going in.'

'Okay.' Regan smiled again and was about to return to the ballroom when the woman took a hesitant step forward. A prickle of unease raised the hairs on the back of Regan's neck. 'Is something wrong?'

'No, I—'

'Have you been crying?' Regan stepped closer to her. 'Your eyes are damp.'

'I'm fine.' The woman sniffed, clearly not fine. 'I just wanted to get a closer look at you.'

During the night many guests had wanted to get a closer look at her, and, while it hadn't been as daunting as she'd first thought, she still didn't like it.

'Why are you crying?'

'I'm Princess Alexa of Berenia.'

'I'm Regan James.'

The woman gave a brief laugh. 'I know.'

'Well, at least I made you smile.' She frowned with concern. 'Has someone hurt you? Are you feeling ill? Why don't I take you back to your table so you can—?'

'No. I don't want to go back to my table.' She gave her a hard look. 'You don't even know who I am, do you?'

Getting an uneasy feeling in the pit of her stomach, Regan shook her head. 'Should I?'

'Considering I was the King's fiancée up until yesterday, I would have thought so. I can't believe he would keep you in his palace and then *marry* you.'

Regan felt as if someone had poked her in the stomach with a sharp stick. 'Do you mean King Jaeger?'

'Who else?' Tears welled up in her eyes again. 'My father thinks you have bewitched him. He blames me, of course.'

'I haven't bewitched anyone,' Regan said vehemently, feeling sick. 'It's just... I mean... I can't explain it to you but I'm really sorry this has happened to you.'

'He loves you. It's obvious by the way he looks at you.' More tears leaked out of her eyes and she valiantly tried to hold them back. 'The way he touches you.'

Regan agreed that he had touched her a little too much. It had kept her in a heightened state of awareness all night. But she knew for a fact that he didn't love her. 'I don't know what to say to you.' Her own emotions felt as if they were being buffeted in a fierce wind. She was at once upset for this woman, who clearly cared for the King a great deal, and incredibly angry at Jag's obvious insensitivity. Why hadn't he told her about his engagement? Why hadn't he warned her that his ex might show up and approach her? Because surely he had known Alexa was invited? He'd signed off the guest list.

'There's nothing you can say.' The Princess raised her regal chin in a show of bravado that only made Regan feel worse for her. 'I tried to tell my father that those photos didn't matter, that you were nothing to the King, but I was wrong.'

'You're not wrong.' Regan bit her lip, anger making her muscles rigid. 'Look, I can't be sure but…maybe things will still work out for you. Maybe you should keep your fingers crossed. You never know what can happen in a couple of days.

But if I were you, and I wanted him as much as you seem to then I *wouldn't* give up hope.'

The Princess looked at her as if she was crazy. She wasn't. She was just really angry.

'Are you going to talk to me at all about what's bothering you or are you going to continue to give me frostbite?'

Regan had been giving him the cold shoulder for the last hour until Jag had finally had enough and called it a night.

'Why have we stopped here?' she asked curtly, brushing aside his question and glancing along the unfamiliar corridor.

'You've been moved from the garden suite to the one adjoining mine.'

She glared up at him, her mouth tight. 'I don't want the room adjoining yours.'

Growing more and more irritated because he'd actually enjoyed what was usually a tedious formal evening, he pushed the door to his room wide open. 'Too bad. The garden suite is now occupied by the King and Queen of Norway. Feel free to join them if you like.'

She looked at him with such venom he thought she'd decide to do it. But then she lifted her dainty nose in the air and swept past him into the room. Sighing heavily, he followed her into his private living room, wondering what had gone wrong in the last hour.

'You don't need to accompany me,' she said; 'I know how to undress myself.'

Jag's eyes dragged down over her lush body and all the way back up. A flush of colour tinged her cheeks and heat surged through his veins. Graphic images of her spread out on his elegant sofa wearing nothing but her delicate gold stilettos drove his frustration levels higher. 'You sure about that?' He shrugged out of his jacket and tossed it across the back of said sofa. 'I'd be happy to lend a hand if you need it.'

'Oh, I'm sure you would.' She folded her arms over her chest. 'I'm sure you've helped many women out of their clothing in your time. Women like Princess Alexa perhaps. Your *ex-fiancée.*'

Ah...suddenly the reason for her cool hauteur made sense. 'Princess Alexa was not my fiancée. Whoever told you that is mistaken.'

'She did,' she said, challenge lighting her golden-brown eyes. 'In between bouts of crying.'

Jag stared at her. He'd spoken to King Ronan personally ahead of the opening dinner, reminding the elderly King that he had never actually committed to marrying his daughter and now he wouldn't be.

'Princess Alexa and I—'

'Please.' Regan held up her hand dismissively, cutting him off. 'Don't feel as if you have to explain anything to me. It's none of my business. I'm only the stand-in. Lucky that you find women so interchangeable, no doubt it's water off a duck's back for you.'

'I *do not* find women interchangeable.'

'No, you just see them as part of a package deal to be moved about according to your needs and political machinations. Is this her ring?' She tugged at the diamond he had given her earlier. 'She stared at it long and hard when she saw it. Did you choose it together?'

'Would you stand still and listen to me?' Her pacing was starting to give him whiplash.

'It doesn't matter. I find I can't abide wearing another woman's ring, even if it is just a prop.'

She held it out to him and Jag gritted his teeth, locking his hands around her wrists and jamming the ring back on her finger. 'That is not Alexa's ring. It is yours. I never chose a ring for Alexa.' Unused to explaining himself to anyone,

Jag found himself in unfamiliar territory. 'A few months ago King Ronan approached me about marrying his daughter. I believed the idea had merit and said I would consider it. In the meantime someone from the Berenian Palace has been feeding information to the Press to create speculation and, I suspect, a way to encourage me to seal the deal.'

'As far as I could tell, it was definitely sealed for her. She sounds as if she's in love with you.'

'I met the woman twice. Do you really believe that's enough time to fall in love with someone?'

She hesitated a fraction of a second before staring down her nose at him. 'Clearly it was for her.'

'I doubt that. The woman is more in love with the idea of being Queen than being my wife, and her father wants easy access to Santara's wealth.'

'I find that hard to believe. She was incredibly upset.' She tugged at her wrists and he released her to put some much-needed space between them. 'But just say your version is the correct one and she's only marrying you for political gain, I would have thought that was right up your alley. No messy emotions involved to muddy the waters.'

His jaw ached from clenching it so hard. Tarik

had pointed the same things out to him the day before. So why, with all the political advantages it also offered, had he killed the idea completely? 'I have explained as much as I am willing to explain to you.'

'Oh, right, because I'm just one of your minions. I suppose you're about to clap your hands next to make me disappear.'

'Don't tempt me,' he grated.

'I think it was really insensitive of you not to tell me about her. You knew that I was nervous about meeting all those people and you just threw me to the wolves.'

'I did not throw you to the wolves. I made sure you were by my side the whole night. And I am not happy that Alexa approached you, but in the end no harm was done.'

'To you maybe,' she said, clearly not placated by his response. 'But that's because you don't care about people. You're so caught up in your duty and your wheeling and dealing you've forgotten the human element. You should make sure you donate your body to science after you die—you'll be the only person in the world who has been able to exist minus a heart.'

'I am not heartless and at the end of the day

this is not about you and me as a couple. We're not a couple. We are a means to an end.'

'Yes, my brother's end.'

Feeling an overload of emotion, Jag walked away from her. 'I refuse to get into this with you.'

'Why?' she volleyed at him. 'Because you're selling Milena off the way King Ronan is his daughter?'

'I am not selling my sister off.'

She gave him a look as if to say 'dream on' and Jag's hands balled into fists. This woman was driving him crazy. 'I'm getting very tired of you questioning my decisions regarding my sister.' He watched as her eyes widened when he paced towards her. 'When Milena was sixteen she became infatuated with an international farrier that had come to work at the royal stables. I assumed it was harmless. I *assumed* he would be a gentleman, given her station and her age. I was a fool. He tried to seduce her even though he was married and he ended up breaking her heart.' He took a slow even breath, anger returning along with his memories. 'Not long after he left she stopped eating and lost an enormous amount of weight. Then I found her with a bottle of sleeping pills clasped in her hand.' He still remembered that feeling of having his heart in his mouth when he'd realised how gravely ill his sister had become, and he'd do anything to ensure that she was never hurt like that again.

'Oh, poor Milena. And poor you.' Regan's sympathy was a tangible force that threatened to wrap around him and never let him go. 'No wonder you're so protective of her. I assumed it was just for political reasons.'

Jag moved away from her so that he couldn't absorb any more of her warmth. 'The political aspect *is* vital. But more than that Milena has always struggled with the need to feel wanted, to feel of value to anyone. She has always blamed herself for our mother's defection. What she fails to realise is that our mother was never maternal. When this marriage arrangement was first presented to me I believed it would give Milena the stability and sense of purpose her life has always lacked. The last thing I need is you coming along and making me second-guess myself.' Shocked to realise how much he kept revealing to a woman who was virtually a stranger, he strode to the windows and stared out at the black, starless night.

'I'm sorry I probably brought back bad memories for you when I refused to eat the other day.' Hearing the deep emotion in her voice, Jag couldn't stop himself from turning to look at her. He'd never met a woman so open with her emotions and so willing to take ownership of her actions. 'And I'm sorry for saying you were heartless. I can see that you really do care very deeply for your sister and it was wrong of me to suggest otherwise.'

'I don't need your sympathy.' Put on the spot by the raw emotion in her voice that paradoxically tugged at his own, Jag put the brakes on the conversation. What he needed was her to get naked so he could work off some of the excess energy coursing through him, not to feel even more than he already did.

He heard her murmur a soft goodnight before she disappeared through one of the closed doors. As he was about to tell her that she'd entered his bedroom instead of her own she returned, red-faced. 'I think I just went into your room. It smells like you.'

Jag's jaw clenched. 'You did.' He pointed to the door on the far side of the room. 'You can access your bedroom through there.'

She ran her hands down the sides of her dress and threw him a nervous smile. 'Okay. Take two.'

Needing to lower his tension levels with something other than her, Jag headed for the bar. He'd just picked up the crystal decanter when she screamed.

Striding through the connecting door, he pulled up short when he found Regan standing on the bed, holding a stiletto sandal in her hand and wearing nothing but a nude-coloured slip. A very short nude-coloured slip.

'Sp-p-pider,' she stammered, her lovely eyes as wide as dinner plates. 'I swear it's as big as a wildebeest.'

'Where?'

'In the…in the wardrobe.'

Finding the offending arachnid, he had to concede that the spider was indeed huge. Maybe not a wildebeest, but if you'd never seen a camel spider before it probably looked as bad as one. Retrieving an empty glass from her bathroom, he captured the spider and tossed it outside the window, closing it after him.

'Technically it's not a spider,' he informed her, returning to find her still on the bed, her long, lithe legs braced apart. 'It's known as a *Solifugae*.'

'As long as it's technically gone I don't care what it's known as. Are there any more?'

Jag checked around the bed, welcoming the diversion from her legs. 'All clear. I'll make sure the staff do a regular sweep of the rooms tomorrow. But rest assured, we don't tend to see very many of them inside the palace. They prefer the open desert.'

'This one got lost,' she said, still warily eyeing the carpet as if she expected to see an army of them come out of the woodwork.

'Come.' He held his hand out to her, even though he told himself not to touch her. 'I'll help you down.'

Still in a state of shock, she took his hand without argument, becoming unbalanced as she stepped off the bed.

Jag caught her in his arms, her body fitting against his like a silken glove, her arms winding around his neck, her legs wrapping around his hips.

Somehow her bottom, round and firm, was cupped in the palms of his hands.

The kiss from the night before spiralled through his head, taking over.

'You wanted to know what I tasted like and now you don't want to repeat it.'

At one point during the night he'd wanted to repeat it so badly he'd nearly cleared the grand ballroom. Part of the problem was that her taste was damned addictive.

The air-conditioning whirred overhead.

Was she breathing?

He wasn't.

Her body was open to his, clinging, her scent winding him up. He was so aroused, he shook with it. All it would take was for him to bunch her silk slip a fraction higher, test her readiness with the tips of his fingers, release himself from his trousers and bury himself deep inside her.

His hands moved to her thighs, tightening on the soft resilience of her skin, then he inhaled raggedly, letting her slide down his torso until her feet touched the floor, biting back a groan.

She stared up at him, as dazed as he was, her eyes dark with unslaked lust. Her nipples were hard, her breathing as uneven as his, and he knew if he put his hand between her legs he'd find she was equally turned on.

A muscle ticked in his jaw. She wasn't here for this. He hadn't asked her to pose as his fiancée so that he could satisfy a hunger for her he was barely able to comprehend. He'd done it to avert an international crisis; he'd done it to get his sister back. How would it look if he threw sex into the mix for the hell of it?

If Chad James was out there having sex with his sister he'd kill him. He'd expect no less in return. He took a step back from her, called himself ten types of a fool and headed for the door before he could change his mind.

CHAPTER SEVEN

REGAN WAS ALREADY up when breakfast arrived on the King's private terrace. She'd showered and changed into her own clothes—jeans and a T-shirt—ignoring the beautiful items the King had provided for her, since she had no idea what would be expected of her today. She thought about the woman who had slipped him her phone number the night before and wondered if he had gone to find her after he'd walked away from her. And then reminded herself yet again that she didn't care.

She stared at the selection of local pastries and fruits and thought about his revelation concerning his sister the night before. She honestly hadn't thought he had the potential to feel anything on a personal level, but after the disclosure about Milena was torn from his chest she could see that he did. He felt things incredibly deeply and she was coming to understand that the way he had coped with taking control of a family and a country so young was to close down his emotions and just get on with it.

She recalled the way he had fed her in the garden suite when she'd gone on a hunger strike. At the time she'd assumed that he'd fed her for purely selfish reasons, but had he done it because deep down he was a nice person? Somehow she preferred the first option. It made it much easier to dislike him if she thought he was a hard-hearted tyrant.

She spied the food now and tried to stop thinking about him so that she could figure out if she was hungry or not when he walked through the glass doors and joined her.

Smoothing the napkin on her lap, she told her heartbeat to settle down.

'You were right last night,' he said quietly, his eyes on her face. 'It was insensitive of me not to have informed you about the situation with Princess Alexa. I hadn't looked at it from your point of view, and I also genuinely believed that Alexa would not be overly disappointed if the betrothal didn't go ahead. I'm sorry I put you in that position.'

Not expecting him to apologise, Regan felt taken aback. 'I probably overreacted a little,' she admitted, knowing that really, she had over-reacted a lot because she'd been unexpectedly jealous of the other woman. Something that didn't make sense at all given their circumstances. 'But it's okay.' She forced a lightness into her voice. 'I told Princess Alexa not to give up hope.'

His brows drew together. 'Why would you tell her that?'

'Because I felt sorry for her. She was really upset and she's perfect for you.' That thought had kept her up a lot during the night. 'She's beautiful and poised *and* royal. In terms of matches you'd make beautiful babies together. You should definitely go ahead with it.'

He moved towards the table and picked up a peach, testing it for ripeness. She hadn't realised how much she wanted him to deny her advice until he didn't. 'You're always looking for the silver lining, aren't you?'

'I prefer silver linings to thunderclouds. Life's tough enough without always waiting to be rained on.'

'That's a romantic way of looking at the world. If you're not careful you'll be blindsided when you least expect it. And you hate surprises.'

'I hate bad surprises.'

'Is there any other kind?'

Well, there was her reaction to his kisses. That was definitely a thundercloud because, as intoxicating as they were, as much as they made her burn for more, she would never be what he was looking for in a woman.

'Good point,' she agreed, frowning as a thought came to her. 'You're not going to say anything to Princess Alexa, are you? I wouldn't want her to get into trouble for approaching me.'

'First you protect my staff, and now the Princess? Who are you going to protect next? Because I don't ever see you protecting yourself and you make yourself vulnerable in the process.'

'That's not true.'

'It is true.' He leant against the table beside her. 'You didn't even realise how much danger you were in that night at the shisha bar, or walking around a strange city alone. Anything could have happened to you.'

'It didn't,' she said, feeling the need to defend herself.

'All evidence to the contrary,' he said, bringing a slice of peach to his mouth. His eyes held hers and the air in the room grew unbearably hot.

'How is it you can eat that and not spill a drop?'

she began on a rushed breath. 'Did you go to a special etiquette school for royals or is it something you're born knowing how to do?'

'I'm careful.'

'Well, if I was eating that I'd have juice all over me by now. When I was younger my mother used to secure a tea towel around my neck whenever I sat down to a meal.' Aware that she was babbling because he made her so nervous, and he was so close, she stopped when he deftly sliced a sliver of peach and held it out to her. 'Open,' he ordered softly.

Open?

Without thinking she parted her lips and the sweet, fragrant fruit slipped inside. Regan's tongue came out to capture it and her heart beat a primal warning through every cell in her body as his eyes lingered on her sticky lips.

Kiss me, she thought. *Please, please, just kiss me before I die.*

'Your Majesty?' A male voice interrupted the awareness sparking between them as brightly as the Christmas lights at Macy's.

Tarik walked into the room, bowing formally. 'Excuse me,' he murmured, seeming to sense that he had interrupted something he shouldn't have. 'You asked me to brief you here and… I did knock.'

'That's fine.' The King recovered from the moment a lot quicker than she did and yet again Regan got the impression that he affected her a lot more than she affected him. 'You didn't interrupt anything important.' He moved away from the table and sat in the seat opposite her. 'What have you got for me?'

'The agenda for the day.' Tarik handed them each a one-page document. 'There have been a few amendments made to yours, sir, that I need to run through with you.'

Jag poured himself a short black coffee and held the pot aloft in question to Regan. She shook her head, hoping that she wasn't blushing in the process. She really had to stop letting him feed her.

'Okay, Tarik, tell me what I need to know.'

The older man ran through a list of morning meetings Jag was required to attend that made Regan feel exhausted just listening to it. 'After the round-table meeting on international banking reform, you're supposed to open the new sports complex at the local primary school followed by a tour of the facilities to drive more economic investment in the area. Unfortunately we've had to reschedule the meeting on foreign policy and counter-terrorism, which you shouldn't miss either, and there's no chance you can do both.'

Jag paused and poured himself another coffee. By the sound of his schedule he'd need to have a jug of the stuff on standby. Regan glanced at her own schedule, which consisted of another day of pampering in preparation for another dinner that evening. She frowned. 'Excuse me, I don't like to interrupt but is there any way I can help out?'

Both men looked at her as if she'd grown an extra head.

Regan rolled her eyes. 'Surely, as your supposed fiancée, I can be of more use to you than window dressing and keeping other men's wives at bay.'

His lips quirked at her attempted joke. 'What did you have in mind?'

'Well, I am a teacher. Is there any way I can do the school tour so that you're free to attend the other meeting? I mean, I would offer to attend the counter-terrorism meeting but other than just tell everyone to love each other I'm not sure what I can offer.'

He shook his head at the incongruity of her comment, his eyes sparkling with amusement.

'What do you think, Tarik?' he surprised her by asking the older man. 'I broke with protocol last night. Would this be stretching it?'

'Not really,' Tarik said slowly. 'I mean, if Miss James were really your fiancée it would be highly acceptable, even delightful, for her to take on a task such as this. It's not as if she needs to contribute anything specific. And her presence would add credence to your pet project, given that you're unable to attend.'

The morning sun glinted off the King's tanned face and made his blue eyes seem impossibly bright. 'Are you sure you want to do this, *habiba*? You know if I'm not there all the attention will be on you and you alone.'

Regan shook her head. 'Pretty much all the attention was on me last night anyway—as you knew it would be. But, as you can't be in two places at once, I'm happy to do it. Seriously, there are only so many times you can get your nails and hair done, and I'm not used to having so much time on my hands. It doesn't sit well with me.'

'If you're sure, then…thank you.' Something

sparked behind his eyes, some emotion that Regan couldn't identify but then he blinked and it was gone. 'Tarik will accompany you. If at any time you think it's too much for you, tell him and he will return you immediately to the palace.'

Jag paced around his room and checked his watch for the hundredth time in half an hour. Regan should have been back an hour ago. Tarik had sent him a text saying they were on their way. So what was keeping them?

About to contact the security detail he had sent along with them, he heard quick footsteps racing down the marble hallway and knew immediately who it was.

Regan burst into the room, her cheeks rosy with exertion, Tarik hot on her heels. They were both laughing at some shared joke and his eyes narrowed. 'Is either one of you aware of the time? We are expected downstairs at the dinner in thirty minutes.'

Immediately Regan stopped smiling. 'It's my fault,' she assured him. 'Tarik told me that I had to finish up earlier but it was really hard to leave.'

'Miss James was magnificent, Your Majesty.'

Jag watched her roll her eyes at his aide in

mocking rebuke. 'That's not true. If anyone's magnificent this man is. I can't believe he's seventy years old. He was kicking a soccer ball around with ten-year-olds.'

'As were you, my lady.'

'I'm just glad I wore flat shoes for the occasion,' she said, pulling the band from her ponytail and letting her glorious mane of hair swirl around her shoulders. 'I'm dead on my feet after today.'

'You're hardly going to be any use to me dead on your feet, Miss James.'

Stark silence greeted his blunt statement and, as Jag became aware that he was experiencing an unexpected jolt of…jealousy…at the obvious camaraderie between his aide and his temporary fiancée, his agitation levels rose. 'I don't remember seeing soccer on the itinerary.'

'It wasn't,' she said demurely. 'Again, that was my fault. We were touring the new gymnasium and sports grounds, which are incredible by the way—hats off to you because I know it was your vision to provide such an amazing space for the kids—and one of the boys rolled the ball my way. I returned it and noticed that the girls were sitting on the sidelines and I encouraged them to join in. Before we knew it we were all playing.'

Tarik was looking at him oddly and Jag drew in a deep breath. 'It's fine. Regan, you need to go and get ready for the dinner. We have...' he consulted his watch '...twenty-five minutes before it's due to commence.'

'Oh, right, of course.' She ran a hand through her hair, tousling it more. 'Oh, Tarik, if it's not too much of a bother, do you mind providing me with the postal address of the school? I have a lot on my mind but I don't want to forget.'

'Of course, my lady.'

'Hold on,' Jag said, feeling his irritation levels rise even higher at their unexpected mutual-appreciation society. 'Why would you need the postal address of the school?'

Regan gave him a faint smile. 'It's nothing. I promised one of the teachers I'd send them some art supplies because it's the one area in the school that isn't flourishing and it's really important.'

'I'm sorry?' Jag was finding it hard to keep up with her.

'The curriculum is really strong on maths, science and English, which can be a bit limiting, particularly for really young kids. They need music and art and lots of time to play so that their love of learning doesn't wither and die in the later years.'

'The reason the curriculum is set up that way is because when I took over as King the school system was in an appalling state.'

'I heard. All the teachers, and local dignitaries, were singing your praises. Apparently ten years ago Santara was in the bottom three percent for literacy and now it's only in the bottom twenty-five percent.'

Jag winced. That was mainly due to the remote country schools that were slow to keep pace with changes made in the cities, but he'd have liked things to be further along than they currently were. The problem was that he couldn't be on top of everything, as Tarik was wont to tell him.

As if reading his mind, his loyal aide raised a brow, seeming to remind him that he wasn't an island, and he scowled.

'Anyway, I said I would send some specialist supplies I know my kids back home love to use.'

Jag shook his head. He should be used to women taking advantage of his position and thinking they could spend his money out of hand. Just because she was spending it on kids didn't make him feel any more generous towards her.

In fact, the disappointment that she was like so many other women, who couldn't wait to get their hands on a man's money, made his tone harsh.

'Next time you think to abuse my generosity and allocate palace funds you might care to run it by me.' His eyes were cool as they held hers. 'I will, of course, honour your promise this time, but next time I won't.'

A heavy silence filled the air and just when he was feeling that he had everything in hand Tarik moved to correct him.

'Your Maj—'

'Tarik, please don't.'

Surprisingly Tarik did as Regan requested and Jag stared from one to the other. 'What were you going to tell me, Tarik?'

Before his aide could speak Regan lifted her eyes to his. 'He was going to tell you that I was planning to pay for the art supplies myself.'

Another silence followed her statement. This time a fulminating one. Jag dragged a hand through his hair. 'How is it that you always seem to wrong-foot me, Miss James?'

'I don't know. Maybe it's because you're always looking for the worst in people.'

'That would be because I've seen the worst in

people.' He sighed. 'And you will not be spending your money on supplies for the school.'

'But—'

'The palace will provide whatever is needed. Education is of vital importance to our nation. Write up a list of what you want and give it to Tarik.'

'Really?' Her face lit up and she gave him a smile that stopped his heart. 'You don't know how happy that makes me to hear a world leader speaking that way about education. Too often governments just pay lip service to education issues and it's completely debilitating for those who work in the industry. Do you have enough funds set aside for musical instruments too? From what I could tell, they're woefully under-represented as well.'

At the term 'lip service' Jag's gaze dropped to her sexy mouth and he reminded himself that he was not an untried fifteen-year-old boy but a grown man in full control of his faculties. 'Don't push your luck, *habiba*.' If she did he wouldn't be responsible for his actions. 'And now you only have fifteen minutes to get ready. Should I tell them to hold dinner?'

'No, no.' Regan pivoted on her light feet and

raced towards the connecting door to her room. 'Give me ten minutes. And thank you. You've made me really happy.'

Swamped by emotions he couldn't pin down, Jag immediately poured himself a stiff drink.

'Everyone loved her today, Your Majesty; she's—'

'Here temporarily,' Jag reminded Tarik, cutting off what was sure to be an enthusiastic diatribe as to Regan's virtues. 'Or have you forgotten that?'

'No, Your Majesty, it's just—'

'I think you're needed elsewhere, Tarik,' Jag informed him, not at all in the mood to hear any more. 'I'm quite sure I can await my fiancée's reappearance on my own.'

'Of course, Your Majesty.'

As soon as the older man departed the room Jag felt like a heel. It wasn't Tarik's fault that the woman was tying him up in knots.

And where the hell was his sister? If she was putting him through this for nothing he'd be furious.

'Okay.' A breathless Regan appeared in the doorway in record time. 'I hope I look all right. Since you're only wearing a suit and tie, I opted for something less formal than last night.' Her hands brushed over the waist of her sleeveless all-in-one trouser suit that faithfully followed the feminine curves of her body, accentuating her toned arms. Her face looked as if it was almost bare of make-up, and her hair fell around her shoulders in a silky russet cloud. 'I didn't have time to put my hair up,' she said, raising a hand to self-consciously pat it into place. 'If you think I should then I can—'

'It's fine.' He cut off her chatter, aware that this was something she did when she was really nervous. 'You look...' incredible. Stunning. *Beddable* '...very elegant.'

Sexual chemistry arced in the space between them, pulling him towards her as if by an invisible pulley system.

She fiddled with her engagement ring and Jag had to forcibly stop himself from reaching for her and wrapping those slender fingers around another part of his anatomy. A stranger to fighting desires as strong as this, Jag found himself growing increasingly frustrated. 'Let's go,' he growled, appalled at how she could arouse him without even trying.

'Okay. Oh, wait.' She stopped beside him at the

door and smiled up at him. 'In all the rush before, I forgot to ask—how was your day?'

How was his day?

Shock made him go so still he could have been nailed to the spot. He couldn't remember the last time he'd been asked that question. Usually people were too busy reeling off a litany of complaints, or asking him to solve problems, to even consider asking him how his day had been.

A lengthy silence filled the room. How was it that this woman managed to uncover weaknesses in him he thought he'd long got over. 'My day was fine.'

'Sorry.' She gave him a faint smile. 'I've upset you again. I always seem to say the wrong thing around you.'

'I'm not upset,' he denied, 'I was just...' He took a deep breath. Let it out. 'Actually my day went very well.'

'Great, then we both had a good day, only...' Her brow scrunched and she paused to look up at him. 'Are you sure everything's okay? You've gone a little pale.'

No, everything was not okay. He was fighting with a very strong instinct to lock her up and throw away the key. And not in the palace this time but some distant location he couldn't get to.

He thought about last night. The roundness of her bottom against his palms, her arms locked around his neck. The chemistry between them had been explosive but he'd possessed enough sanity at the time to know that doing anything about it would produce a list of regrets that would rival his inbox.

He felt his insides coil tight as the need to have her tried to edge out logic and reason.

As if she sensed the direction of his thoughts her throat bobbed as she swallowed, her eyes wary. As they should be. Because nothing good could come of constantly thinking about how much he wanted her and so he ruthlessly clamped down on emotions that he didn't want to feel, and needs he didn't want to have, and focused on his duties for the night. 'Everything's fine,' he finally said, directing her towards the door. 'Let's not keep my chef waiting any longer. His retribution isn't worth it.'

CHAPTER EIGHT

STANDING ON THE back steps of the palace balcony as the last of the summit delegates boarded a helicopter, Regan let out a long sigh. Presumably her duties as the king's escort would be over now that the four days were up, and she wondered why she didn't feel better about that.

For the past two days she had barely seen Jaeger. They had crossed paths only at social functions when he required her company, but always he seemed distantly polite and at the end of the evening he had done little more than bid her goodnight before heading to his office to do even more work.

She couldn't escape the feeling that he had been avoiding her a little, which had suited her fine. Spending time with him only gave her a false sense of connection with him that she didn't want to feel. Already all he had to do was look at her to make her burn, and she hated the fact that her senses had been awakened by a man who couldn't make it any plainer that he didn't want her. And why would he want her when she was merely a means to an end for him?

Wondering what would happen next given that their missing siblings had not yet returned she steeled her spine when he detached himself from the small party he was speaking with to approach her, his expression serious.

'I know the summit is officially over,' he began, 'and that our deal only extended to today, however there is one more obligation that is required of you.'

'Obligation?' She forced herself to sound as composed as he did. 'Is this to do with Milena and Chad? Have you located them?'

Yesterday the security detail searching for Milena had reported that there might have been a sighting of her and Chad in a hiking store in Bhutan five days ago. It had eased Regan's mind because Chad was an avid hiker, but it still begged the question that if the two of them were merely hiking why hadn't they been more open about the whole thing?

'No I have no new information on our missing siblings,' Jag said grimly. 'This is a business obligation. The President of Spain is thinking about investing in our agricultural infrastructure. He wishes to see how he might utilise it in his own country and I have organised a short trip to the interior of Santara. As his wife is accompanying us, it would seem strange if you stayed behind. Particularly since she tells me that you have bonded over the past few days.'

'Yes, she's lovely.'

His head cocked to the side, his eyes curious. 'She also tells me that you speak fluent Spanish. Why didn't you tell me that you speak another language?'

'You didn't ask.'

Annoyance briefly pulled his brow together. 'I'm asking you now. How is it that you live on the East coast of America but have come to speak Spanish? It's not as if the language is prevalent there.'

'My mother was a Russian immigrant. She could speak five languages and spoke them often at home. I picked up my love of languages from her.'

'Does that mean you speak Russian too?'

Regan nodded. 'And French and German. Though my German is really basic. I wouldn't want to put it to the test.'

His eyes gleamed as he looked at her. 'A woman of hidden talents.'

Regan glanced at a pair of butterflies as they flitted over a row of flowers hedging the expansive lawn area, the admiration in Jaeger's eyes making her chest tight. The strain of hiding her physical reaction to him over the last few days was wearing her down.

'We will be gone most of the day. I suggest you wear something light and loose. The interior of my country gets very hot.'

Regan watched him stride away from her, immediately feeling a sense of deflation. She supposed it was to be expected since she felt as if she'd been on a roller-coaster ride since she'd arrived in Santara. It was as if she was living someone else's life. It didn't help that her feelings for the King were all over the place. One minute she didn't want to see him ever again, and the next she wanted to plaster herself all over him.

Back in her room she scanned the elaborate wardrobe Jag had provided for her, choosing camel-coloured trousers and a long-sleeved white linen shirt. Remembering the spider from the other night, and knowing they would be outdoors, she ignored the more delicate open-toed sandals and shook out a pair of her own white running shoes. Tying her hair into a low ponytail, she waited for Jag to return. When he did he looked ruggedly masculine in low-riding jeans, boots and a lightweight shirt similar to hers.

'Do you mind if I bring my camera?'

'Of course not. As long as you don't post any photos of me on social media.'

'No fear of that.' Regan grimaced self-consciously. 'I've learned the consequences of that particular lesson.'

His gaze turned thoughtful as he stopped beside her. 'Has it been so bad, *habiba*? Being here with me?'

Regan blinked. He could ask that after ignoring her for the last two days?

Fortunately she was saved from having to find an answer to his question when one of his bodyguards informed him that their helicopter was ready for boarding.

Never having taken a helicopter ride before, Regan was thrilled. Once they had left Aran her eyes were riveted to the vast expanse of sand dunes that stretched in peaks and valleys in an endless sea of gold and brown. In the distance she could see rocky mountain ranges with hints of green, and tiny villages dotted here and there. Jag sat opposite her and she felt his curious eyes on her. She listened as the two other occupants chatted about the sights but didn't join in, enjoying the sound of Jag's voice coming through the headset now and then as he pointed out some of the more interesting aspects of the countryside. At one point she nearly jumped out of her skin when he tapped her on the knee and said her name at the same time. Her eyes flew to his, her heart pounding even at that small contact, to find him pointing out of the window on her other side. 'Camel train,' he said and Regan couldn't contain a smile as she spotted the line of over twenty camels meandering across the top of a distant dune. He grinned back at her and for a moment the connection between them was so strong it was as if they were the only two people in the world. Then Isadora, the First Lady, fired off some questions in rapid-fire Spanish and Jag answered.

As they neared their destination Regan was amazed to see miles and miles of brilliant green fields. Jag explained how the ground was watered by both underground springs and the water that ran off the mountains. An engineering team had devised a revolutionary method for storing the water so that it didn't evaporate in the harsh sun that was a year-round issue for the desert nation.

Landing, they had lunch and took a tour of the various garden centres before the President asked if they could also stop at Jag's nearby thorough-bred stables. Climbing into a cavalcade of SUVs, they were once more whisked through an ever-changing landscape towards the stables.

Not being a horsewoman, Isadora was taken into the main house to rest from the harsh rays of the sun, while Regan headed to the stables, declining an invitation to join the men in the fertility clinic. She wandered from box to box, petting the muzzles of the horses she met and taking photos.

'Oh, you're a beauty,' she crooned as she came upon a giant white stallion, snapping off another photo. She grinned as the horse angled his head. 'And a real poser.' She laughed. The stallion snorted at her from the rear of the box, his black eyes studying her intently.

'You must be at least sixteen hands high,' she praised him. 'Come on. Come say hello.' The stallion stamped his foot a couple of times and then dropped his head, moving towards her and nuzzling her palm, inhaling her smell. 'I wish I had a carrot to give you,' she murmured, leaning in and breathing his horsey scent deep into her lungs.

'Actually he prefers sugar.'

At the sound of Jag's voice the horse whinnied and lifted his head. Man and horse eyed each other like long-time friends.

'I see you've become mesmerised by Miss James's soft touch,' he said, putting his hand in his pocket and pulling out a sugar cube. Instantly the horse nuzzled his palm, devouring the treat.

'He likes that,' Regan said, laughing when the stallion bumped her shoulder, urging her hand back up to his nose. 'You're a demanding thing,' she murmured, happily acquiescing and caressing beneath his mane where the hair grew as silky as duck down.

'Like his owner,' Jag said, his eyes following the movement of her fingers as she combed them through the horse's mane.

She wanted to ask him why he was suddenly paying her attention again, but the gleam in his bright blue eyes made the words die in her throat. Instead she asked, 'What's his name?'

'Bariq. It means lightning.'

The horse whinnied and Regan laughed. 'And I'm sure it suits you,' she assured him.

'He doesn't usually take to strangers so readily. You must know horses.'

'Yes.' Her throat thickened. Horse riding had been one of those things they had all done as a family when her parents had been alive. An activity that had stopped when her parents had become sick. She leaned into the stallion's neck and breathed him in. 'I love horses.'

'Why does that make you sad?' Jag asked softly.

Embarrassed at having given herself away, Regan shifted uncomfortably. 'It was my parents' favourite pastime. They used to take Chad and me riding as often as possible.'

He frowned, his finger lightly tapping the bridge of her nose. 'You have one or two new freckles.'

Regan rubbed at the place he had touched. 'Deft subject change, Your Majesty,' she said with a small smile. 'Unfortunately the freckles come with the hair colour.'

'Not unfortunately. Your colouring is as warm as your personality.' His voice had roughened and sent sparks careening through Regan's body. 'And I don't like to see you sad.'

Not knowing what to say to that, Regan focused on the stallion. Why didn't he like to see her sad? She was only a means to an end for him, wasn't she?

'Good afternoon, Your Majesty.' A man in a groom's uniform strode down the blue stone aisle towards them. 'Would you like me to saddle Bariq for you to ride?'

Jag hesitated, his eyes on her. 'Care to take a ride with me, Regan?'

Regan immediately shook her head. 'I don't think so… I haven't ridden in a long time,' she admitted huskily.

'I guessed that, *habiba*,' he said, his eyes soft. 'But there is nothing to worry about. I'll be with you the whole time.'

'What about the President and his wife?'

'He is joining his wife for iced tea, after which they will be returning to the airport, where their plane is waiting to return them to Spain. I said goodbye on your behalf.'

Unable to think of another reason to not take this moment to enjoy herself, Regan smiled shyly. 'If you're sure?'

'I am.'

Twenty minutes later, having changed into

jodhpurs and a fitted tunic, Regan waited with barely leashed excitement to mount her horse, a lovely palomino mare called Alsukar. Or sugar.

It had been more than a decade since she had ridden but she remembered it as if it were yesterday, bittersweet memories of shared family time filling her head.

'Okay?' Jaeger pulled up alongside her, his magnificent white stallion snorting and champing at the bit in his eagerness to gallop.

Jaeger barely tightened his hands on the reins, his deep voice alone enough to bring his prancing horse under his control.

'Yes, I feel like Bariq. I can't wait to get going.' A groom gave Regan a leg-up into the saddle. Regan took the reins and felt the energy of the horse beneath her.

She couldn't contain her smile. She was looking forward to testing her riding legs, and creating some new memories that were not entirely based on the loss of her parents. And then she wondered if Jaeger had suggested they ride for precisely that reason and told herself not to be fanciful. He had done this for no other reason than that his stallion needed a run, and she'd be a fool to entertain any other notion.

Before moving out Jag brought his horse close to hers. Leaning over, he shook out a piece of cloth and proceeded to fashion it on top of her head into what he told her was a *shemagh*. 'When we get outside you take this piece and tuck it into here so that it covers your mouth and nose.'

His fingers grazed along her jaw as he fixed the headdress into place, sending a cascade of shivers across her skin. Sensing her reaction, Sugar shifted sideways and Jag grabbed hold of her bridle to steady her.

'Thanks,' Regan said, not quite meeting his eyes.

He nodded and then proceeded to expertly fold his own royal blue *shemagh* that perfectly matched his eyes. He was a visual feast and she wondered what it would be like to be able to truly claim this man as her own.

They rode across oceans of sand dunes, taking the horses through their paces, and giving them their head from time to time. Jag tempered his horse to stay by her side and she felt sorry for the big stallion, who just wanted to gallop.

Finally they stopped to rest at a small watering hole on the outskirts of a village. Regan dismounted on jelly legs and immediately went to one of the guards who had trailed them to retrieve her camera from his pack. Completely enthralled by the humble beauty of the place, she snapped off a few photos of the contrasting colours and textures surrounding her.

A few locals came out of the low-lying buildings, bowing low when they saw who had arrived to greet them.

Jaeger was clearly a revered leader, greeting his people with kindness and respect.

Born to lead, he had said, or words to that effect, and, seeing him in action, as she had done over the past four days, she knew it was true.

A group of local men approached Jaeger and the two guards that had followed them dismounted and joined their King.

Regan snapped a photo of the impressive trio, raising her brow when he looked at her.

Is this okay? her look enquired.

Fine, his slight nod replied.

Feeling happy, she turned to find two young girls approaching her, carefully carrying a tray full of clay mugs. They curtseyed and offered one to her.

Taking the cup of cool water gratefully, Regan smiled. *'Shukran.'*

'*Shukran, shukran,*' the young girls tittered, dancing away as if they couldn't believe she had taken their offering.

She watched as they approached Jaeger, bemused at how beautifully he handled their shy attention, taking a mug and bowing to them in return.

Regan couldn't prevent the smile on her face, hot colour stinging her cheekbones as he looked across at her. Could he read her thoughts? Did he know how much she was enjoying herself with him? Did he know how hard it was for her to remember that she was only here with him like this because Chad and Milena were missing? That he believed Chad had committed a crime in running off with his sister?

Not wanting to dwell on any of that now, she turned back to the vast open space of the desert, the light breeze moving gently across the sand like a whisper. Enthralled by the deep quiet of the land, she raised her viewfinder again. When Jaeger came into view across the way she paused. He had unwound his blue *shemagh* and it framed his handsome face, giving his skin tone a golden-brown hue. Curious, she watched an old man approach, handing Jag an enormous bird of prey.

The bird made a noise in greeting and clung to Jag's gloved hand. As wild and untamed as its master, its proud profile perfectly mirroring Jag's.

Regan felt her breath catch. He really was the most magnificent creature, and before she could stop herself she depressed the shutter and snapped a round of photos.

A small crowd had gathered around him and he released the bird into full flight, watching as it soared into the air on ginormous wings. Jaeger gave a short, sharp whistle and the magnificent bird swooped and dived above them, putting on a magical display. Regan couldn't take her eyes off either man or bird as they worked together in perfect harmony, the bird circling high and waiting for Jaeger's commands before plummeting to earth like a bullet from a gun, completely trusting that the King would provide a safe landing for it. Which he did, without even flinching as those huge talons wrapped around his thick leather glove.

As if sensing the lens on him, Jaeger turned in her direction and stared at her, his features proud, his blue eyes piercing as if he were gazing directly into her soul. Regan depressed her finger on the shutter again, her lens capturing the moment before she lowered the camera. She swallowed as he continued to look at her, completely captivated by the heat and masculine energy that emanated from his riveting gaze. It was as if she had become the prey and he were the falcon, with her firmly trapped in his sights.

The memory of his fingers threading through her hair, cupping her face as he kissed her, thrusting his tongue into the moist heat of her mouth, made her breath catch in her throat. It was so easy to imagine him coming to her now, bending to her and kissing the breath from her body, tasting her with his tongue, and gripping her waist in his powerful hands, telling her everything he wanted to do to her. Then doing those things…

One of his men spoke in his ear, breaking the spell between them, and Regan realised it was time for them to ride back. The sun had already started to sink towards the horizon, the heat of the day also starting to ebb away.

Handing the falcon back to the old man, Jag made his way over to her. 'You look flushed, *habiba*,' he said softly. 'I should have given you a wide-brimmed hat as well.'

Regan felt flushed but she knew it had more

to do with the scorching hot images of the two of them together than the sun. Safer, though, to have him believe that her heightened state was to do with mother nature than for him to realise that she couldn't look at him lately without wanting him.

'How did you find the ride?' he asked, adjusting the front of her *shemagh*.

'Wonderful.' She shaded her eyes from the sun as she looked up at him. 'It was truly wonderful.'

'No sad memories?'

'At the start but... I didn't realise how much I miss being around horses until now so...thank you.'

'It was my pleasure.'

'That bird—'

'Arrow?'

'Fitting name,' she said. 'He's magnificent.'

'*She's* magnificent. I found her as a chick at the base of a cliff when I was out riding years ago. She had fallen from her nest and wasn't ready to fly. The mother could do nothing for her and there was no way I could scale the side of the cliff to return her to her nest so I took her home with me. We've been firm friends ever since but I hardly get time to take her out any more. She wanted to hunt today but I didn't think you would want to see that.'

'What does she hunt?'

'Mice, hares, smaller birds.'

'Spiders?'

Jag laughed. 'Don't sound so hopeful, *habiba*.'

At the memory of the giant eight-legged monster in her wardrobe, Regan scoured the ground around them. 'You're safe. From creepy crawlies.'

His amused eyes grinned into hers and Regan felt the intimacy of the moment even though they hadn't even touched. For a split second she wondered if he was about to bend down and kiss her. And she wanted him to.

'We need to leave. It is getting late.'

'Of course. I can see the sun already dipping down towards the horizon and it gets cold in the desert at night. Or so I've heard.'

She was babbling, she knew it, and, by the way his lips tilted up at one side, he knew it too. 'It does. The desert is very unforgiving. It is not a place you want to get caught in during the day or the night.'

'Okay, well...'

'Sire, your horse.'

Thankful for the interruption, Regan turned

blindly to the man who had brought their horses. Or, rather, Jag's stallion.

'What happened to my mare?'

'She grew tired from the ride out. She will be stabled here for the night and one of the men will return for her tomorrow.' Jaeger collected the reins from the man.

Placing a sure foot in the stirrup, he swung himself up onto the enormous horse, reaching his hand down to her, palm facing up. 'You will ride with me.'

Ride with him? No way. She was trying to lower her awareness of him, not elevate it into the stratosphere. 'That's okay.' She gave him a wan smile. 'I can...' She looked around, hoping to see some other mode of transport at her disposal.

'I'm afraid the A train uptown has left for the day.'

Regan laughed. 'Was that a New York joke, Your Majesty?'

'A pretty lame one,' he admitted unselfconsciously. 'Come. Give me your hand.'

Regan stared up at him. Everything inside of her said that she should not do this. That she should insist that he find another way for her to make it back to the stables. Maybe with one of his trusted guards, but she knew she'd be wasting her breath and really…just the thought of riding with him atop that massive horse gave her goosebumps.

She moistened her lips and placed her hand in his. Right now, out here in the desert, where it was wild and free, she felt very unlike her usually cautious self.

Jaeger's hand closed around hers and seconds later he had her seated on the horse behind him. He twisted around to face her, adjusting her *shemagh* once more so that it covered most of her face. Regan's heart beat fast as she stared back at him, so close she could smell the combined scent of horse and man. It was quite the aphrodisiac. She couldn't see his expression because his sunglasses were back in place, his own *shemagh* drawn across his face. He looked like the dangerous outlaw she had imagined him to be when they met and a thrill went through her. Back then her instincts had screamed at her to run. Now they were begging her to draw closer.

'You'll have to hang on tight, *habiba*. Bariq likes to have his head.'

Before she could respond Jag whirled the stallion on his hind legs and raced them out of the small village and across the sand, giving Regan no choice but to comply with his suggestion or fly off the back of the horse and land on her rear end.

Determined to remain steadfastly immune to his proximity, she lasted about five seconds before she became aware of the lean, hard layer of muscle at his abdomen as her fingers flattened across his middle. Remembering what those muscles looked like without his shirt led to thoughts of sex, and the harder she tried to banish the word from her mind the more it stuck until it was all she could think about.

Between that and the smooth, powerful motion of the horse, she was decidedly rubber-legged when they arrived back at the stables.

Jag dismounted, his blue eyes hot and stormy as he looked up at her with his arms outstretched. Regan automatically swung her leg over the saddle, holding herself still in the circle of his arms as she waited for her legs to be firm enough to hold her upright.

Not wanting to meet his eyes in case he read every single hot thought she had ever had about him, she focused on the front of his shirt, glad when one of his bodyguards strode over and handed him a phone.

Thankful for the reprieve, she stroked the sweaty sides of the stallion's neck, telling him how big and strong he was.

'Careful, *habiba*, you don't want it to go to his head,' Jag mused as he turned back to her. 'This is supposed to be one of the fiercest horses in the land but he looks as if one word from you would send him to his knees.'

Regan smiled. 'He looks fierce because I suspect people have always been scared of him, but all he needs is to hear how amazing he is.'

Jaeger quirked a brow. 'Don't we all?'

Regan paused. Was that what Jaeger needed? To hear how amazing he was?

'That was Tarik. He has just informed me that the tribe of my ancestors has invited us to attend a congratulatory dinner tonight.'

Regan blinked at him. 'Because the summit is over?'

'No, because I have decided to take a bride.'

She stared at him blankly and he let out a rough laugh. 'You, *habiba*.'

'But we're not really going to be married!' she said, shock sending her voice high.

'To them we are.'

Regan shook her head, frowning. 'I'm not sure it's wise for me to meet even more of your people.' She shook her head, compelled to state the obvious. 'I mean, I'm not your fiancée. I'm a pawn. We both are because I'm using you to ensure Chad doesn't spend the rest of his life in some dungeon, and you're using me to get Milena back.'

A muscle flickered in his jaw, the one that worked every time he got angry. 'I don't have a dungeon,' he growled.

Before she had time to react he caught her face in his strong hands and raised her lips to his. Momentarily stunned, Regan stood there, her body flush against his. It wasn't a gentle kiss, or an exploratory kiss. It wasn't even a nice kiss. It was hot and demanding, skilfully divesting her of any willpower to resist. Not that she was trying to.

Instead her arms hooked around his neck and she rose up onto her toes, meeting the sensual onslaught of his attack with a hunger as deep as his own.

At her total acquiescence he groaned, shifting her so that she was pressed between him and the stable wall, her head tilted back so that she was his to command. And he did, softening the kiss, taking her lips one at a time before plundering her mouth with his tongue.

Her lips clung to his, a sob of pure need rising up inside of her. This was what she wanted, what she needed, what she had craved ever since he had kissed her and touched her that night in the garden suite. This thrilling throb of desire that she had only ever experienced in his arms. It was like a fever in her blood, a rush of sensation that couldn't be denied.

And then it was over just as quickly as it had begun. Once more he pulled back and she was left panting and unsteady, her body aching and empty.

She heard him curse as he turned his back on her. Then he spun towards her, breathing hard.

A groom exited a nearby stall carrying a tack box and Regan wondered if that was why he'd stopped.

She glanced up to see Jag watching her and for once he didn't seem completely immune to what had just happened between them.

'I think that should clear up any misconceptions you have that I didn't want a repeat of our kiss the other night.'

She blinked up at him, shocked at what he had just disclosed.

He looked shocked himself and shook his head. 'Wise or not, we have to attend the dinner tonight. It would be an insult not to, since we are already in the region. We will spend the night at my oasis and return to the palace first thing tomorrow morning.'

'Your oasis?'

'The place I come to when I want to unwind.'

CHAPTER NINE

WHEN WAS HE going to learn that kissing her was not the way to expunge her from his system?

He shook his head and strode inside his Bedouin tent. Set on the edge of a private rock pool and surrounded by palm trees, it was an upscale version of those his ancestors had used to live in. Usually he felt a sense of peace wash over him as he shed the suits and royal robes to reconnect with the man beneath, but not tonight.

He yanked his shirt over his head and made his way to the purpose-built shower at the back. He should not have let her words anger him, he thought savagely; that had been the problem.

He wasn't used to someone questioning the wisdom of his decisions and he didn't like the reminder of how they were using each other even though it was true. Riding Bariq back to the stables with her tucked against his back hadn't done his nerves any good either. If at any time she had shifted her hand an inch lower she would have realised that the only thing on his mind was sex.

Wondering how she was finding her own accommodation and whether she was wishing it was a five-star hotel, he donned a white *thawb* and royal headdress and went outside.

The sun was low on the horizon, his favourite time of day in the desert, the ambient light turning the sky a dusky mauve. Hearing a sound behind him, he turned to see Regan dressed in a brightly coloured *thawb* and flowing floor-length headdress. As soon as they had arrived at the village a group of local women had descended upon their future Queen to give her a traditional makeover. The results were stunning. She was completely covered from head to toe, and yet she managed to look like an exotic treat waiting to be unwrapped. Her chin tilted upwards in a tiny gesture he had first assumed was haughtiness, but now realised was one of self-consciousness. Despite her fair skin, she looked as if she was born to be here. Born to be his.

Perturbed by that last thought, Jag didn't realise he was frowning until Regan raised a brow. 'I did try to tell them to stop with the black kohl and henna. I look like I'm dressed for a Halloween party, don't I?'

Jag felt instantly chagrined at her pained expression. 'You look stunning. I just had something else on my mind.' Such as the fact that he might be slowly losing it.

'Well, whatever it was it obviously wasn't nice. Which is hard to believe when you're in a place like this.' Her gaze swept across the small cluster of tents and the deep blue lagoon. 'This is like something out of a fairy tale.'

'You don't wish for more modern accommodation?'

'Are you kidding?' Regan gaped at him. 'People pay a fortune to have experiences like this. I had no idea tents had carpets and real beds.'

'You're getting the upscale version. Come. It is a short drive to the village.'

'We're not going by camel?'

Jag couldn't prevent a grin at her teasing comment. 'I draw the line at some traditions.'

He held the door wide and her sheer veil caught on his arm as she made to step into the car. As he lifted his hand to disengage it his fingers caught around her silky hair and he nearly threw caution to the wind and buried his hands in the sexy mass and brought her mouth up to his again.

Moments later their car pulled up alongside a large purpose-built marquee. Inside low tables were set in a wide circle with cushions scattered throughout the tent for seating, soft music playing from the edge of the entertainment area.

He watched Regan as she greeted his local tribespeople, speaking softly and attempting a few words in his native tongue, her adept mind already picking up a few phrases. He remembered the way her face had lit up when they had ridden first in the helicopter, and then on horseback through the desert. He had half expected her to hate his homeland but to his surprise she had seemed enamoured by it.

As his people were fast becoming enamoured by her.

'Your Majesty, your table.'

The tribal chieftain guided them to the central spot in the marquee, where everyone would be able to watch him and Regan interact.

Seeing the smiles on his people's faces was like a punch in the stomach. He hadn't given much thought to how much they wanted this to be real and he conceded that Regan had been right to be hesitant in accepting the invitation. Probably he could have got out of it but once again he found himself making a decision to keep this woman close when it wasn't necessary.

He frowned. What was necessary was getting back to the palace and to what was important—work and finding Milena. But before that could happen he had tonight to get through.

'How are you feeling?' he asked Regan softly. 'Overwhelmed? Nervous? I should apologise because you're the centre of attention again.'

'I'm fine.' She gazed around the wide, brightly decorated space. 'Maybe you dragging me to your palace has been good for me. I think I've become a bit reclusive at home, keeping to my usual routine and never stepping outside of my comfort zone. My world is so small compared to yours. I don't know how you do it; having to be switched on all the time.'

'Sometimes it's tough,' he admitted, something he'd never said out loud before. 'Sometimes I'm presented with problems and challenges with no clear answers, and I find that the hardest of all.'

Especially now that Regan had started making him question his relationship with his siblings. Did Rafa stay away from Santara because Jag had not created a clear role for him at the palace? Had Milena run off with Chad James because she didn't want to go through with her royal marriage and couldn't tell him?

'We don't always get it right,' she said softly, as if reading his mind.

But he did. He had people depending on him. People who needed him to get it right. Especially when his father had been too caught up in his domestic dramas to lead the country as it deserved to be led.

Fortunately the tempo of the music increased, cutting off any further chance of conversation. A good thing, since he had a habit of revealing too much of himself around this woman.

Dancers poured into the tent, smiling and clapping, and, despite her misgivings about being here, Regan decided she was going to enjoy the evening. It wasn't as if she was likely to get a chance to experience something like this again any time soon. And yes, it would be better if she wasn't so aware of the man beside her, but there wasn't much she could do about that. Try as she had…

They might not have met in the most conventional of circumstances, but the way her body responded to him was one hundred percent *conventionally* female.

And knowing that he was just as attracted to her was driving her crazy. It made her wonder what might have been if he had been an ordinary guy she had met at her local park. But he wasn't. He was a king, a man of supreme importance— and her brother had run off with his sister.

She gave an inward groan, wishing that Chad would return, wishing that this crazy situation was over so that she could go back to normal. If that was even possible after the way Jaeger had touched her, kissed her…

A kaleidoscope of butterflies took flight in her stomach as she absently watched his strong hands as he gestured with the person next to him. His wrists were thick, his forearms sinewy and dusted with dark hair. Everything about him was so potently male it made her feel breathless with need.

I'm falling for him, she realised with a jolt of dismay. *I'm really falling for him.*

She must have made a small sound of distress because he immediately turned towards her, his eyes scanning her face.

'*Habiba*, what is it?'

Regan shrugged helplessly. 'Nothing.'

His frown told her that he didn't believe her but he was prevented from asking more when she joined in the energetic clapping as a troop of new dancers took to the floor. This time the group was made up entirely of women in brightly coloured outfits and carrying sheer scarves.

You're not falling for him, she assured herself sternly. You're suffering from a serious case of lust for a man who knows how to kiss a woman into a stupor. You're not the first, and you certainly won't be the last, to imagine themselves in love with the sheikh. Princess Alexa was a good case in point. She'd met the King twice and fallen for him. And maybe Jag was right in that the Princess only wanted to marry him for political reasons, but Regan had her doubts. She'd seen the woman's heartfelt misery in thinking she had lost him.

Blindly she turned back to concentrate on the dancers. The women were undulating their hips with practised ease, gracefully weaving silken scarves around their bodies in a coordinated display of confidence and femininity. Combined with the lyrical music, it was both provocative and sensual. But all Regan could really concentrate on was the man seated so closely beside her.

Glancing at him through her lashes, she noticed a fine line of tension bracketing his mouth. She wondered why he was having such a reaction to the beautiful display when the story behind the dance hit her on the head. This was no ordinary dance. The scarves, the hip bumps, the sensual spell that held the crowd captivated…this was a type of love dance.

One of the performers broke from the circle and Regan held her breath, only to release it again when she approached a young woman, encouraging her to join her on the floor.

The woman did, smiling shyly at the young man she had been seated next to.

The crowd cheered and clapped encouragingly.

'Please tell me they're not going to expect me to go up there?' she whispered raggedly.

Jag's blue eyes snagged with hers and she knew the answer before he even opened his mouth.

She shook her head. 'I'm a hopeless dancer. I have no coordination at all.'

'You forget I've seen you on horseback, so I know that's blatantly untrue.'

'Riding a horse is nothing like dancing. At least

with horseback riding if something goes wrong I can blame the horse.'

Jag laughed. '*Habiba*, I—'

Before he could finish one of the dancers undulated in front of her, beckoning to her. By this time three other women had joined the dance, mimicking the sensual movements in a joyful display of passion and love.

Oh, God, she was seriously going to die of embarrassment.

Jag's eyes were a deep blue as she slowly rose to her feet. His hand caught hers. 'Regan, you don't have to do this.'

It was kind of him to say so, but Regan knew she'd be disappointed in herself if she didn't do it. Not only because she would be disappointing the people watching, but also because it was another chance to step outside her comfort zone and own it.

'I'll be fine,' she murmured with more bravado than she felt, throwing him one last beseeching look, and she followed the dancer out onto the floor, accepting the rose-coloured scarf that was offered to her.

At first she felt rigid and clumsy, conscious of everyone watching her, but slowly, and by some miracle, the sensual music started to flow through her, luring her to lower her inhibitions.

Telling herself to stop being a coward, she raised her arms and twined her hands together above her head, undulating her hips slowly. The crowd clapped and the music throbbed in time with her heartbeat. Laughingly, she tried to emulate the movements of the other dancers. And then she just let go, closing her eyes and giving herself up to the moment.

Unbidden, Jag's tender kiss against the stable wall invaded her head. Her breasts rose and fell at the memory of his hard body pressed to hers, his mouth devouring her, tasting her, arousing her. A sweet lethargy spread through her limbs and she made the mistake of opening her eyes and staring directly into his.

It was like being torched by an open flame. The heat and hunger in his gaze was so intimate it took her breath away. His whole body transmitted unmistakable masculine desire and it seared her to her core.

The scarf floated teasingly in the air between them as she mimicked the earlier movements of the women, the delicate fabric wafting in front of him. With lightning-quick reflexes he grabbed hold of the end, bringing her to a standstill.

She couldn't do anything but stare at him, and then, as if in slow motion, he started to reel her in.

Regan was completely undone to see the delicate skein of silk wrapping around his big, tanned hand, the sight somehow enhancing his potent masculinity when it might have diminished it in a lesser man. But there was nothing lesser about Jaeger al-Hadrid and Regan knew that once she reached him there would be no turning back.

'Regan.'

His eyes were as hot as the sun, his rough tone pure sex.

Regan's breath hitched in her throat. There was only one thing she could say to that look.

'Yes.'

Understanding completely that the word hadn't been a question, he unfolded lithely to his feet. His height dwarfed her, the *thawb* making him seem even more powerful than usual. As soon as he stood the music stopped, but really Regan only vaguely registered the change.

He took her hand and not a single sound was uttered as he led her from the tent.

Once they were outside, the cool night air was a welcome relief against her heated cheeks but it did nothing to relieve the hot, pulsing desire that thrummed through her and turned her insides liquid with need.

When they reached his black SUV he dismissed his driver with a single nod.

Regan hesitated beside the open passenger door, forcing her eyes to meet his. 'I need to know one thing,' she said, her voice breathless with longing. 'Are you going to stop again and pull back from me?' Because if he did she didn't think she could bear it.

His large hand rose to cup her face, his thumb brushing along her cheekbone, his eyes as dark as the night sky above them. 'I've tried that. It doesn't work.'

A quiver went through her at his rough, gravelly tone. She gave him a tremulous smile and his fingers tightened against her scalp. 'Jump in.'

The big car flew across the desert road, eating up the distance between the marquee and his private tent in no time. Neither of them spoke, the air in the car so thick it made talking impossible. It made thinking impossible too and then he was beside her door, opening it, his warm hand pressing to the small of her back as he guided her towards the large tent she knew to be his. He raised the flap and she moved inside, suddenly nervous, the sound of it dropping back into place behind them like the crack of a whip in the stillness.

His hands framed her face and for a heartbeat he just looked at her. Then he lowered his head and took her mouth in a kiss of devastating expertise.

Regan could feel her heart racing, her body turning to liquid.

The kiss, slow and gentle at first, quickly turned urgent. He tasted of wine and coffee, and a deep male hunger that fed her own.

The only thing she managed to whisper was his name but that must have been enough because suddenly she was being lifted and he was carrying her towards the rear of the tent. He placed her on the edge of the enormous mattress, taking a moment to reef his robe off over his head, leaving him in low riding cotton pants that left little to her imagination.

Her lips went dry as he stood before her, gloriously male, from the thick muscular arms and shoulders down to his lean hips and long legs.

'I won't stop this time, *habiba*, not unless you want me to.'

Regan's heart hammered inside her chest. Maybe she should stop, maybe she should say no, but she couldn't. Spending time with him these past few days, watching him command a room, seeing his quick mind in action, and then today, the way he handled Bariq and Arrow, seeing his gentleness with those less physically capable than himself, was… He was everything a woman could ever hope to find in a man and she loved him. Completely and utterly; as scary as that felt. 'I don't want to stop. I want this. I want you.'

She knew her words held a deeper meaning than he would attribute to them, and suddenly she was aware that this might not be the smartest decision she had ever made.

He lifted his hand to her, beckoning, and she no longer cared about being smart.

'Then come to me, Regan. Let me show you what you do to me.'

CHAPTER TEN

JAG COULDN'T CONTROL the shudder that went through him as Regan gracefully rose from the bed and came towards him. He wasn't sure how he had restrained himself thus far but he forced the aching need riding him hard to subside. He didn't want to impose himself on her or scare her with the strength of his desire. He wanted her to come to him as his equal. As a woman who wanted him regardless of how they had met, or why they were together. He needed her stripped bare because it was exactly how she made him feel.

She stopped a pace away from him, her eyes luminous in the soft light, the silky floor-length veil she still wore framing her beautiful face.

He lifted his hands and searched out the pins that held the veil in place until the fabric pooled at her feet, leaving her glorious hair unadorned.

'Turn around,' he instructed, his voice hoarse.

Silently she complied and he lowered the zipper

in the back of her *thawb*. She wasn't wearing a bra and his blood surged at the sight of her pale, slender back. His fingers traced a line down her delicate vertebrae and back up, rejoicing in the tremor that went through her.

'Cold?' he asked, his hands sweeping her hair aside and lowering his head to the tender skin where her neck and shoulder joined.

'No.' She shook her head, resting it back against his chest. He smoothed the gown over her narrow shoulders and held his breath as it too slithered to the floor.

'Then turn around, *ya amar*. Let me see you.'

Slowly she did as he instructed, her little chin lifted ever so slightly as she stood before him in only a tiny pair of black panties and delicate sandals.

He had been with many women in his life. Women he had admired and even liked, but he had never been with a woman who created in him this deep, gnawing hunger to possess, to brand, to claim as his own for ever and beyond.

Shaking off the sensation that he was in much deeper than he'd ever been before, Jag drew her closer. 'You're beautiful,' he said, his eyes memorising every sensual detail of her supple body;

her straight shoulders and slender torso, the rise of her round breasts, high and firm, the narrowness of her waist, and the subtle flare of her hips and long legs. Hips designed to cradle a man's body, legs designed to wrap around him and hold him tight. 'Perfect.'

Unable to hold himself back, he gathered her close, groaning as the tips of her breasts nestled in the hair on his chest. She arched into him, her hands grasping his shoulders to pull him even closer. 'Kiss me, please.'

He did more than that, he devoured her, taking her mouth in a long, searing kiss that was a promise to how he intended to possess her with his body.

She made a soft keening sound, her hands kneading and caressing his naked shoulders. Jag dragged his hands down her ribcage, sweeping along her spine, before bringing his hands to her breasts. He cupped them gently, plucking at her tight nipples between his fingers.

She moaned deeply, arching against him, her body rising to his, climbing his until she was fully in his arms with her legs wrapped around his waist, her breasts inches from his mouth.

He gave a husky laugh. '*Habiba*, how very nice

to meet you.' He leaned forward and cut off her answering chuckle by taking her nipple into his mouth. She clung to him, crying out in an agony of pleasure. He wanted to give her that pleasure. He wanted to give her everything.

He suckled her gently, flicking her nipple. Her thighs tightened around him as her arousal heightened and he rewarded her responsiveness with firmer and firmer pulls of his mouth. First on one breast then the other.

'Jaeger! Jag!' She writhed against him and he sensed she was close to climaxing. The knowledge sent his own arousal into the stratosphere.

'Regan, I—' He cursed as he laid her on his bed, his movements clumsy with his own imminent loss of control.

Shaking, he tried to steady himself, but she reached up to frame his face as he came down over the top of her, pulling his mouth back to hers.

'Wait,' he growled as her fingers trailed down over his muscled back and slipped beneath the waistband of his trousers. She was driving him to the edge of control and he needed to pull back for a moment, centre himself. But she didn't listen, her mouth opening wider under his, her tongue gliding into his mouth to mate with his, her clever fingers shattering his ability to keep a part of himself back.

'I don't want to wait,' she murmured against his neck. 'I need you. I need you inside me.'

'If you don't wait,' he growled, 'this is going to be over before it's begun.'

'I don't care. I need—'

He grabbed her hands and shackled them above her head with one hand. With the other he ruthlessly divested himself of his clothing. 'I know what you need.'

He came down over the top of her, pressing her into the mattress. She parted her thighs and her hips rose to meet his.

'Dammit, Regan, I need to see if you're...' He'd been going to say *ready for me*, but he had already discovered the answer. 'Regan.' He positioned himself over her, his legs nudging her thighs wider.

'Yes. Please, Jag, do it.'

Her fingers dug into his hips and he surged into her, completely sheathing himself inside her.

She gasped and he instantly stilled. He smoothed her hair back from her forehead, putting his weight on his elbows. 'Okay?'

Breathing heavily through her mouth, she nodded. 'You're just so... Oh, that feels fantastic.'

He flexed again and felt her body go liquid around him. Then he stilled.

'Protection.' How in the world had he forgotten that?

She shook her head. 'We don't need it. I'm on the Pill and I've only been with one other man. Years ago.'

One other man?

'And I trust you.'

It was those last words that made his heart leap inside his chest and tipped him over the edge. Or perhaps it was the way her inner muscles rippled around him, drawing him further inside. Either way he no longer cared. All he cared about, all he could think about was taking them both higher, driving them deeper until time and space became irrelevant.

'Jag!' Her body gripped him tighter, growing taut as she moved more frantically beneath him.

'That's it, *habiba, ya amar*, like that... Yes, just...'

He felt the instant her body reached its peak, revelling in the way she screamed his name as she came apart in his arms. And then he couldn't think at all because her muscles were clenching around him like a silken fist. His body surged forward, driving into her with none of his usual finesse, until, with his own cry of release, he lost himself inside her.

Jag woke some time later to find Regan wrapped around him like ivy. One arm slung over his chest, her thigh positioned high over his. He couldn't remember the last time he'd slept all night with a woman. Sleep was a luxury he usually caught in snatches. Was that what had woken him so suddenly? The fact that he wasn't up? Or was it the warm, naked woman at his side who had given him more pleasure than he could ever remember having in bed?

His flesh stirred, definitely liking that second idea better than the first.

She must have registered the change in him because she made a small, sleepy noise, her body snuggling deeper against his.

Jag smiled, shifting a strand of her hair back from her forehead. He loved her hair. The colour, the texture… It felt like silk and fairly vibrated under the sunlight.

He told himself that he wouldn't wake her. She

deserved to sleep and she would no doubt be a little tender from not having made love in such a long time.

She had only had one lover before him. He'd had no idea she was that inexperienced but he wasn't unhappy about it. Had he ever had a woman who had given herself to him so openly? So *wholeheartedly*? It was as if she'd held nothing back from him and he wasn't sure he entirely liked how that made him feel. Vulnerable. Open. A little raw, perhaps.

Slowly he became aware of his heart beating and knew it wasn't a sensation he registered very often.

Regan shifted again, her arm moving as if she was searching for something in her sleep.

Him?

Heat coiled through him.

On some elemental level Jag recognised that Regan had unlocked a deep-seated hunger inside him he wasn't altogether comfortable with. She made him think of things like loss and longing, like desire and need, and...

'The heart knows what the heart wants.'

Zumar's statement came to him from out of nowhere.

The heart?

This wasn't about his heart. It was about sex. Very good, very hot sex.

His hand tightened in her hair as she made another little sleepy sound. It was meant to reassure her that everything was okay but deep inside he wasn't all that sure that it was true. 'It's okay, *habiba*, you're only dreaming.'

'Jag?' Her brown eyes fluttered open, dark and confused in the pre-dawn light. She leaned up on one elbow, her lovely autumn hair sliding across one shoulder, the hint of jasmine and sunshine drifting between them.

'Is it morning?'

'No.'

They stared at each other. Common sense asserted itself, warning him to back away, to put some distance between them.

Obviously picking up on his thoughts she frowned. 'I should go back to my tent. You must want to sleep.' She swallowed, her eyes darting from his, presumably searching for the gown he had dumped on the floor.

Jag wanted to tell her that was a really good idea. The best idea. But he couldn't because it was neither of those things.

'That's a terrible idea, *habiba*,' he said, his voice husky.

Rolling her beneath him, he clasped her hands above her head. 'Especially when I have many more delicious plans for you.'

She gasped as their lower bodies connected, the uncertainty in her eyes replaced with a burning hunger that matched his own. She softened beneath him, her lips raised to his. He didn't hold back, sealing his lips over hers and swallowing her groan of pleasure with a deeper one of his own.

Nudging her thighs apart with his knees, he entered her in one smooth, deep thrust.

'Oh!'

Her eyes went wide, her lips parting.

'*Oh* is right.' He kissed her temple, her eyes and along the side of her jaw. She whimpered beneath him, her lips seeking his 'You're so beautiful, Regan. The sexiest woman I have ever met.'

'Jag.' His name was a sigh against his neck, her arms enfolding him, holding him to her as her hips moved under him.

Without warning he deftly rolled them both until he was on his back and she was held over him.

Her glorious hair fell around them. He moved

it back, finding and cupping her breasts. She moaned, her head falling back on her neck. Using only his stomach muscles, he levered upwards and drew one of her nipples into his mouth. Her arms clasped around his back.

'Oh, I like this position.'

Revelling in her enjoyment of their bodies, he surged upwards, taking her hips in his hands and moving them both closer and closer to a place he knew he'd never been with any other woman.

Regan depressed the shutter button on her camera and hoped that she'd captured the moment the two hawks flew side by side in a perfect mirror of each other.

Hearing footsteps behind her, she glanced over her shoulder as Jag crested the small rise above the oasis.

A week ago if someone had told her that she could be so uninhibited with a man in bed, so relaxed, she would have laughed in their face. But there was something about this man that made her feel free and able to be herself. Maybe it was his inherent honesty and desire to do the right thing. It spoke to her and made her want to reciprocate in kind.

BOUND TO HER DESERT CAPTOR

All morning she had refused to let herself over-think things as she was wont to do. What was the point? They had shared an incredible night of amazing sex and that was that. Yes, he had asked her to spend the day with him at his oasis, but again she wouldn't overthink it. The fact was, the man worked like a Trojan, he was entitled to a day off and this was his place to come and unwind. And if he wanted to spend time with her... well, that was nice, but he'd made his position about relationships and love clear from the start and, even though she could guess that those beliefs were driven by parents who hadn't loved each other or their kids enough, it didn't change anything.

It would be beyond arrogant for her to imagine that she could be the one to change him.

And what would that even mean anyway? That she would upend her life and move to Santara and really become his queen? She nearly snorted at the thought. Yes, those things happened to some people, but it was a one-in-a-billion chance, and it took both parties to want it. At the end of the day Jag didn't think love was important and she thought it was vital. And of course, there was still the issue of their siblings to sort out...

'Can I see?'

He gestured to her camera and she handed it to him. 'Go ahead.'

A lock of hair fell forward over his brow and she let out a sigh at the sudden urge she felt to push it back.

He paused on the photo she had taken of him with Arrow on his arm, his eyes staring at her.

'I wanted to know what you were thinking when I took that,' she said, her voice husky.

He looked up, his eyes intense, and for once she hoped he couldn't read what was on her mind. It would be beyond embarrassing if he realised she had fallen hopelessly in love with him.

'I don't remember.' He adjusted her *shemagh* and handed her camera back. 'You're very good.'

'You don't need to say that. You've already got me into bed.'

He gave a short burst of laughter at her dead-pan comment, hauling her against him for a quick kiss. 'I never have any idea what you're going to say next. But I meant it.'

Regan shook her head. She knew her limitations as a photographer and it didn't bother her. 'Which goes to show that the almighty King of

Santara doesn't know everything after all,' she said with a smile. 'I'm no Robert Doisneau.'

His eyebrows rose. 'Robert Dois—who? Is this someone I should be worried about?'

Regan laughed. 'No. He's a famous photographer from last century. When I was a teenager I became enthralled by a photograph of two lovers kissing on a Parisian sidewalk. It was one he had taken. There's a magic to it, a sincerity. The couple look so in love…it's as if they can't wait to get back home and had to kiss in the street or die.'

And suddenly Regan realised why she spent so much time photographing couples. They satisfied a deep longing to find the kind of love her parents had shared and which she feared she'd never experience. Unfortunately making love with the King of Santara had created the same longing inside of her.

She gave a little laugh at the improbability of it all. 'I've always wanted to take photos like that and go to Paris. Neither one has happened yet.'

'Both still could.'

'Paris, maybe. Some day. But photography, no. I'm a teacher now and I love my job. I love inspiring kids to learn, and one of my joys is taking a special photo of them during the year and presenting it to them on their birthday. They love it. And I'm not convinced that being a professional photographer would give me the same level of satisfaction. Oh, look, the hawks are back.' She shaded her eyes as she watched their majestic antics. 'Or are they falcons? I can't tell.'

'Hawks.' He watched them with her. 'Falcons are smaller but have a longer wingspan. And falcons grab their prey with their beaks, whereas the hawk uses its talons.'

'*Ouch.* Fortunately they don't seem hungry right now. Look, they're circling each other.'

She raised her camera and started clicking away right when their talons joined together.

'Oh, wow, did you see that? They're dancing.' She couldn't suppress the smile on her face.

'They're not dancing, *habiba*,' he said roughly, his eyes on her mouth. 'He wants to mate with her.'

Regan's breath caught at the raw, elemental hunger in his gaze as he looked at her.

'Falcons mate for life,' he continued. 'And once they've established a home they never stray from it.'

Regan's throat went thick. 'That's so lovely.'

They both watched the birds skim across the top of the blue lagoon. 'Now, that looks lovely.' His hands found her waist and he lowered his head to hers. 'Come swimming with me.'

Much later Regan lay with her head in his lap, shaded by the huge palm trees bordering the pool, the breeze gently rustling the fronds overhead.

Jag held a small piece of something or other to her lips.

'Try this—you'll like it.'

Regan opened her eyes to look up at him. 'You have to stop feeding me. I think my stomach is going to burst.'

'Just one more,' he said lazily, tempting her. 'You know I like feeding you.'

Regan felt herself flush with pleasure. Being with him that morning and afternoon had been wonderful and, despite her better judgment, she had let herself soak it up. Let herself soak him up.

They'd made love twice more, once in the lagoon and then again on the blanket. He'd done things to her that made her body instantly tighten with anticipation but she knew reality would set in again soon.

'What are you thinking about, *habiba*?'

'You,' she said honestly.

He gave a purr of appreciation, his thigh muscle tensing beneath her cheek as he shifted. He prowled over the top of her, his powerful arms and shoulders flexing as he moved. 'Anything specific about me?'

She ran her fingers through his hair, loving the way his eyes darkened to almost black as he looked at her.

'That you're not as scary as I first thought you were.'

'Not as scary, huh?'

'No.' Happiness surged inside her as he gazed at her with wicked playfulness. 'You're like a big domestic pussycat when it comes down to it.'

'Is that so?' She gave a squeal of delight as he flicked her sarong aside and lightly tickled her ribcage. 'Want me to show you how much of a pussycat I am?'

The sensual intent in his eyes was unmistakable.

'Are you sure no one can see us?' she asked, breathless with longing.

He nuzzled her breast, tugging her nipple into his mouth. 'I'm sure.' He licked her and tortured her until she was a mass of pure sensation. 'I told you this place is totally off-limits to anyone else.'

'Your own private paradise,' she husked, reaching to touch him anywhere she could.

His smile turned sexy as he kissed his way down her body. 'I think that's what I might start calling you,' he murmured, parting her legs so that he could press his tongue high along the inside of her thigh.

Regan cried out, gripping his shoulders, her insides pulsing with sensual anticipation of his wicked touch.

'My own private paradise,' he agreed, dipping his head to take her to her own private paradise, and leaving her wondering how she was ever going to get over him.

What must have been at least an hour later, given the placement of the sun, she woke to find Jag sitting on a nearby rock and staring out at the water. She took a moment to study him, drinking him in so that later, when he was no longer around, she could recall exactly how he looked. The feeling was at once bittersweet and utterly frightening.

As always, he sensed her eyes on him and turned to her. Their eyes met and for a moment they just stared at each other. Shockingly, the connection between them was almost more intimate than the sex. She blushed, wondering what thoughts were going through his mind, but she was too cowardly to ask. He wanted her; she knew that without a doubt, so she was determined just to enjoy it for what it was.

He held out his hand to her and a small smile tilted her lips. She loved the way he did that, offered her his hand as if it was the most natural thing in the world. As if she was the most important person in the world to him.

A rush of emotion made her fingers uncoordinated as she fixed the sarong over her breasts and tried to untangle the knots in her hair formed by his nimble fingers. When she reached him he slowly drew her to him and wedged her between his legs, her back to his front. She felt him bury his face against her hair and breathe deeply. Warmth suffused her and she turned, lifting her face for his kiss, when his phone rang.

Grimacing with annoyance, he reached around her and pressed the button. Regan heard an outpouring of Santarian and felt the immediate tensing of his body.

Slowly he disengaged them and strode across

the sand. Watching him, Regan knew instantly what had happened even before he turned to her, a coolness in his eyes when before there had only been heat and need.

'They're back, aren't they?'

He nodded. 'Time to get dressed.'

CHAPTER ELEVEN

A HEAVY SILENCE permeated the helicopter ride on the trip back to the palace, making it seem interminable. Jag appeared to be as caught up in his thoughts as she was in hers, neither one of them making any overtures to the other. It was as if the lover she had spent the day with had vanished, to be replaced by the cold man she had met at the bar. Gone was the domesticated pussycat indulging her in endless pleasure by the side of the lagoon.

A sense of rising dread churned her stomach the further they flew, her feelings divided between wanting Chad to be okay, and concern over what had happened and how that would impact on the man beside her. She wondered if Jag remembered the deal they had struck. She knew that he would honour it. But then what?

With expert precision the pilot landed on the helipad and Jag jumped to the ground, only absently reaching back to assist her to duck beneath the whirring overhead blades.

He strode ahead of her up the path towards the rear of the palace, and Regan finally got to experience what it felt like to walk two paces behind him. Or maybe four. Quickening her pace, she barely noticed the decadent scent of the magnolia trees that lined the path, or the velvet dark sky above.

Jag pushed open a heavy set of doors at the end of a long corridor, his stride not faltering as he strode up to his sister and enfolded her in his arms.

He held her to him for a long moment. A lump rose in Regan's throat and then her eyes sought out the other occupant of the room.

'Chad.' His lanky frame looked as hale and hearty as always and she rushed over and hugged him tightly. 'I've been so worried.'

Chad hugged her back. 'Me too.'

The hairs on the nape of her neck prickled and she turned to see Jag staring at her brother.

Tension rocketed into the room like an incoming sandstorm. 'You have a lot to answer for.'

'No.' Milena placed her hand on Jag's arm. 'Don't blame Chad. It was all my idea.'

Jag's thunderous expression returned to Milena. 'What exactly was all your idea?'

'It's a long story.' Milena sighed. 'And I'm sorry I worried you. I know I did the wrong thing but I felt as if I had no choice. But first...you're engaged...' Her lovely eyes fastened on Regan. 'Is that right? Chad said it wasn't possible, but you're wearing the most important family heirloom in the collection, so it must be.'

Shocked, Regan stared down at the beautiful ring before lifting her eyes to Jag's, only to find his eyes completely devoid of emotion.

'Regan?' Chad stared at her hand. 'How is this possible?'

Regan shook her head, her brain struggling to keep up with the fact that Jag had trusted her not to lose something so precious.

'There are more important things to discuss,' Jag cut in coldly. 'Like, *where have you been*?'

Milena's face went pale as he bellowed at her, clearly unable to handle her brother's wrath.

'I think we need to calm down first,' Regan suggested quietly. 'They're both safe and home. That's the most important thing.'

As well as her getting this ring off her finger and back in a vault.

'Stay out of this, Regan,' Jag rasped with icy precision. 'You will not influence how I deal with this.'

She felt Chad bristle beside her. 'I don't think you should speak to my sister that way.'

'I'm not interested in what you think.' Jag turned his lethally sharp gaze on Chad. 'And you're lucky she's here. If she wasn't you'd already be in jail.'

'Jag!' Milena cried.

'One of you had better start talking,' he grated. 'And if you have compromised my sister in any way, James, you'll be sorry you ever set foot on Santarian soil.'

'As you have compromised mine!' Chad burst out.

'Chad!' Regan stared at him. As he had grown up he had become as protective of her as she was of him, but she'd never experienced him coming to her defence so avidly before.... 'You have no idea what you're talking about.'

'Don't I?' Her brother puffed out his chest. 'There's obviously something going on between the two of you. I can tell by the way he looks at you.'

By the way he looked at her?

Right now he was looking at her as if she were chewing gum stuck to the bottom of his shoe.

'What has happened between myself and Regan is not your concern,' Jag advised with a killing softness. 'What has happened between you and Milena is.'

'That's your opinion, Your Majesty, but I can't believe my sister would be with you of her own free will.'

'Chad, stop,' Regan implored him. 'Don't make this about me. You've been gone for two weeks. Of course the King wants answers. So do I.'

'I feel terrible,' Milena mumbled. 'This is all my fault. Please, Jag; Chad isn't to blame.'

Regan watched him run a hand through his hair, clearly trying to rein himself in for his sister's sake. Her heart went out to him because she knew why he'd been so worried about her. 'Why don't you both sit down and tell us what happened?'

Chad threw Milena a quick glance but was wise enough not to approach her.

Milena cleared her throat. 'I'm sorry if I've caused a big mess, Jag, but I couldn't go into my marriage next month without having some time to myself.'

'You did this for time to yourself?' Jag thundered.

'No. Not just that.' Milena looked to Chad for reassurance. 'I just wanted to feel normal for once. No bodyguards, no photographers, no having to be polite all the time. I know you won't understand this because it all comes so easily to you, but sometimes I don't think I know who I am.'

'Milena—'

'No, let me finish,' she said, taking a deep breath. 'Chad and I have grown close over the last few months and…when I told him my plan to take a secret holiday he insisted that he come with me to make sure nothing happened to me.' She threw Chad a quick smile. 'I knew it would be a mistake, but I also thought that if you knew I was with a friend you would worry less. I was only hoping you'd find out it was a male friend after we returned.'

Jag's expression told her that it hadn't made an ounce of difference, but Regan heard the note in Milena's voice that said that she'd been hoping to return in triumph, presumably so that she could prove to her over-protective big brother that she had grown up. Unfortunately such a tactic was likely to have the opposite effect. Milena winced at Jag's continued silence. 'I guess not. But please, don't blame Chad. If anything, you should be thanking him for being there for me. I didn't even know how to buy a train ticket!'

'I would be thanking Mr James if he had come to me with your hare-brained scheme instead of sneaking off and foiling my attempts to find you. Do you have any idea what would have happened if anyone had got wind of your disappearance? If the Prince of Toran had?' He paced away from her. 'It's only fortunate for us that he expects Santara to take care of all the wedding arrangements. If he'd once tried to call you—'

'I knew he wouldn't.'

'That's beside the point.' Jag turned to stare at Regan's brother. 'Tell me, just how close have you become?'

'Not as close as you and my sister,' Chad ground out.

'Chad, please,' Regan admonished. 'Don't make this worse.'

'How can my stating the obvious make things worse? I've been without internet access this past week, and when I reconnected I nearly died seeing photos of you and him together. You're everywhere in the news, do you realise that?'

She hadn't because she hadn't been given any access to the internet herself. 'I'm sure it's nothing.'

'Nothing? It's not nothing. Ask the King.'

Regan's eyes flew to Jag's. He stared back at her and she saw that he knew how big this had become and that he hadn't cared. The only thing he'd wanted was for Milena to come back and now she had. 'Chad, it's not important. I agreed to do it because we both wanted you to return to Santara.'

'You both agreed to what?' He looked from her to the King and back. 'To becoming engaged to him? My God. I can see it's true. Please tell me you didn't sleep with him for that as well.'

'Chad!'

Ignoring her, he glared at the King. 'How could you involve my sister? She had nothing to do with any of this.'

'I don't think you're in a position to question me,' Jag growled softly.

Before her brother could get any more aggravated and say something really stupid, Regan stepped in. 'I came to Santara to look for you, Chad. No one forced me to do that.'

'Why? I sent you an email explaining that I would be out of reach.'

Regan narrowed her eyes. 'The last time you told me not to worry I got a call from the police precinct to come and bail you out.'

'I was sixteen!' he exclaimed. 'And this is a completely different thing.'

'Yes,' Jag interjected coldly. 'It's far worse. And you should be thanking your sister, not haranguing her. If she wasn't here you'd be in a far worse position than you currently are.'

'I don't think—'

Jag turned on him then, using his formidable height and years of authority to silence her brother. 'No, for a smart man you didn't think.'

'Chad, please,' Milena pleaded. 'It will only make things worse and it's all my fault.'

'It's not your fault,' Chad corrected. 'It's that you live under the reign of your autocratic brother, who never takes anyone's needs into consideration except his own.'

'Okay, enough.' Regan stood up. 'Jag is not like that and you clearly have no real understanding of the worry you've both caused by sneaking off together.'

'Just tell me.' Jag pinned her brother with his icy gaze. 'Did you compromise my sister?'

Milena gave a shocked gasp. 'Jag—'

'Silence,' Jaeger snapped at his sister. 'You are betrothed to be married to a very important man. If you've slept with Chad James I need to know.'

'She hasn't,' Chad bit out, facing the King with his shoulders back. 'Your sister is a beautiful person and I would never take advantage of her like that.'

Regan heard the protective way Chad spoke about the younger woman and stared at him. *Was he in love with Milena?*

'We didn't do anything like that, Jag,' Milena said crossly. 'Chad was a perfect gentleman. If you're going to be angry then be angry with me.'

'Don't worry,' Jaeger bit out. 'I'm furious with you.'

'I'm sorry,' Milena said, tears forming at the edges of her eyes. 'I was really desperate and I thought you'd say no if I asked.'

The stark truth of that flashed across the king's taut features. 'Who else knows about this?' he asked stiffly.

'Only Chad.'

Jag nodded curtly. 'You look exhausted. We will talk more about this in the morning. Mr James, you will not leave the palace until this situation has been officially resolved.'

'What are you going to do to him?' Milena asked.

'That is not your concern.'

Milena leapt to her feet, her small fists clenched. 'Dammit, Jag, sometimes I wonder if you're even human any more.'

'Milena!'

His harsh call stayed her exit, her slight body vibrating with tension. She didn't turn to look at him. 'Permission to leave your presence, Your Majesty.'

The muscle in Jag's jaw clenched tight. Regan's heart jumped into her throat because she could tell by the flash of emotion across his face that he had taken Milena's words to heart. No doubt he felt responsible for everything that had happened, and she knew he wouldn't welcome her attempts to make him feel better about that.

'Go. We'll talk more in the morning.'

'Don't expect me to go anywhere without my sister,' Chad said.

Jag gave him a faint smile. 'I would expect nothing less.'

Finally he turned to face Regan. 'I believe this is when you say "I told you so".'

A lump formed in her throat, her hands trembling. 'I don't want to say that.'

What she wanted to say was that she loved him, that she wanted to be with him, that she understood his anger, and wanted to be the one to soothe it, but knowing that he had never wanted anything like that from her held her silent.

'Gracious of you. But this is definitely the time I apologise for inconveniencing you. I was wrong.'

'I don't want your apology,' she whispered fiercely. What she wanted was for this formal stranger to disappear and bring back the lover she had known at the oasis.

His gaze seemed to take her all in at once, and then there was nothing. It was as if he had closed down every emotion he'd ever had. 'Mr James, please follow me.'

Regan felt shell-shocked by Jag's departure. Was he coming back after he'd talked to Chad? Or was that it?

But of course that was it. The reason she was

even here had been resolved. His sister was safe and the summit was over. Did life just return to normal for him now?

A breath shuddered out of her body and she clamped her arms around her waist. Was it that easy for him? That simple? But then, what had she expected? It had always been going to end when Chad returned. She'd known that. All day she'd reminded herself of the same thing and had convinced herself that she was just taking it for what it was. Well, now was the time to prove that. He'd told her that practice helped him contain his emotions and, well…now would be the time for her to try that too.

Only she wasn't so sure she could move on from him that easily. She'd fallen in love with him. It was exactly the scenario she had feared. Falling for someone who didn't want her back. It was almost as if she'd willed into being the very experience she'd spent years avoiding. But then, fate had a way of making you face your worst fears. She should have known that. And what was the mantra after you faced your fears and survived? You'd be stronger for it?

A sob rose up in her throat and she stifled it. That might take a while.

An hour later someone knocked at the door of the garden suite and she immediately assumed it was Chad.

It wasn't, it was Tarik. He smiled at her soberly and handed her a document.

Regan scanned it. It was a press release stating that her engagement to the King was over. It completely exonerated her of any responsibility, merely stating that after careful consideration she had decided to return home.

'If you're happy with the wording, my lady, the King asks that you sign it.'

Regan nodded, her heart in her throat. 'That was fast.'

Tarik handed her a pen. 'His Majesty likes to work that way.'

'Yes, I know,' she said, moving to a table and scrawling her signature at the bottom. She took a deep breath and wondered if the buzzing noise she could hear was inside her head, or outside.

'His Majesty has also given you a settlement for inconveniencing you but said that if it wasn't enough to name your price.'

'His Majesty is very keen to see me go,' she said softly, wondering if he would renew his engagement to the Princess Alexa now that he was free. It seemed unlikely but then this world wasn't her usual one. Royals made deals and arrangements in the blink of an eye. 'And Chad?' she asked.

'Chad is here,' a voice said from the doorway.

Regan glanced up at him blankly and then felt her resolve start to crumble. 'Oh, Chad!'

He stepped into the room and she raced into his arms.

'I'll leave you alone now, my lady,' Tarik said courteously. 'If there is anything you need, please let me know.'

'Wait, Tarik, there is.' She pulled away from Chad and tugged at the diamond on her finger. It resisted her initial attempt to remove it, but with enough force she worked it free. 'Please return this to His Majesty.'

'The King said that you were to keep it.'

The lump in her throat got bigger. 'No.' She shook her head to hold back tears that suddenly sprang up behind her eyes. 'It's not mine to keep.'

'As you wish, my lady.'

Regan nodded. 'And thank you.' She gave him a watery smile. 'It was nice to get to know you.'

Tarik nodded, bowing as he slowly turned to leave.

'Wow,' Chad said, releasing a long breath. 'This is really full-on.'

'What did you expect?' Regan asked. 'Did you really think you could go off with Milena and there would be no consequences?'

Chad sighed. 'I suppose I didn't really think about the consequences. Milena is a princess. If anything, I thought that once she returned everything would be fine and go back to normal.'

'Wrong.'

'Oh, Reggie, I can see you're upset. I'm sorry you got dragged into all of this.'

'It's okay.' She sniffed knowing that it was very far from okay. 'I'm fine.' It was the way it had always been in the past: her taking care of Chad, not the other way around.

'No, you're not. You look like you're about to cry.' He gave her a wan smile. 'I'm truly sorry. I had no idea that you would rush over to Santara to try and find me.'

'I probably should have stayed home in hindsight but… How did your meeting with the King go?'

Chad made a face. 'He pretty much bawled me out over what I'd done.'

'I don't doubt it. He was worried sick about his sister. It was pretty irresponsible.'

'It didn't seem like it at the time. But he didn't ball me out so much over Milena as over you.'

'Me?'

'Yeah, he dragged me over the coals for scaring you the way that I did. Told me I had to take better care of you.'

'Oh…that was…' She took a breath. It was typical of a man who took his familial responsibilities seriously is what it was. 'He's a decent person when you get to know him.' Funny. Sexy. Strong. Smart. 'And you? What happens for you next?'

'King Jaeger has ordained that I am allowed to continue to work for GeoTech if I want to, but I'm to have no contact with the Princess ever again.'

Regan heard the slight strain in his voice and groaned. 'You're in love with her, aren't you?'

'In love with her?' Chad looked at her, astonishment widening his eyes. 'Of course I'm not in love with her, we're just friends. I mean, she's incredibly beautiful inside and out but…honestly, she reminded me a bit of myself at the same age. When I felt unsure about my place in the world.' He grimaced at the memory. 'I felt bad that she didn't have anyone supportive in her life the way

I had you and I wanted to be there for her. But right now I'm more worried about you.' He took her hands in his. 'Did the King hurt you in any way? Did he force himself on you? Because if he did I'll… I'll—'

'He didn't force me, Chad.' She gave his hands a reassuring squeeze before moving towards the windows overlooking the garden. 'Not in the way you mean. He was just incredibly worried about his sister. I might have done the same thing he did if our situations had been reversed.'

A sort of pained silence followed her statement and she glanced over to see Chad watching her. 'You're in love with him aren't you?'

Regan gave a shuddering smile. 'Is it that obvious?'

'Oh, Reggie. What are you going to do?'

'Nothing,' she said. 'There's nothing I can do. He's made it more than clear that he wants me gone, so I guess I'll go home.'

'Have you told him how you feel?'

'God, no.' Regan gave a resigned shake of her head. 'Believe me, Chad, if King Jaeger had wanted me to stay with him he would have said so. But the fact is he has everything he needs already.' And all she had to do was find a way to get over him.

'There's a car waiting to take me back to my apartment. Do you want to come with me?'

'Of course. It's not like I have anywhere else to go.'

'But the King… Are you going to at least say goodbye to him?'

Regan thought about it but she knew she couldn't do it. 'He knows where I am, Chad, and he knows I'll be going with you. Prolonging the inevitable isn't going to change anything.' In fact, it would only make her feel worse.

CHAPTER TWELVE

JAEGER LOOKED DOWN at the report in his hand that detailed just how phenomenally successful the summit had been. It was everything he could have hoped for and yet he had to force himself to feel enthusiastic about it. He'd had to force himself to feel enthusiastic about anything since Regan had walked out of his life a week ago.

It was as if every day was a test of his endurance. A test of his stamina.

He recalled the day the phone call had come through about his father's accident. At first the words coming out of Tarik's mouth had been surreal and then his brain had kicked into high gear. He'd made sure Milena was taken care of. Then he'd flown home to Santara and been met by a legion of cabinet ministers and officials, all awaiting direction on how to handle the death of the King and what to do next. It had been an immense learning curve, and Regan had been right when she'd said that he hadn't grieved properly.

He'd been almost numb through those first difficult months and by the time he might have had some time to take a breath it had seemed indulgent to do so. He had a job to do and he'd done it to the best of his ability.

He'd thought *that* had been the greatest test of his stamina. Turned out it was nothing compared to watching Regan get into that car with her brother without a backward glance.

But what else had he expected? He'd scared her in the shisha bar and then again in her hotel room, he'd forced her to come to the palace, where he'd detained her, then he'd forced her to play hostess for him at an international summit, after which he'd forced her to go to his oasis and… His mind blanked out the events that had taken place in his bed after the celebratory dinner his tribesmen had put on. It had been the only way he hadn't jumped on a plane and immediately followed her to New York. But he hadn't forced himself on her that night. He knew she had come to his bed willingly, her ability to deny the chemistry between them about as strong as his had been.

Zero.

But what was the point in reliving it all? She

was back in New York, back to her normal life, and so was he. Back to…back to…

A knock at the door prevented his brooding thoughts from continuing. Thank the heavens.

Tarik entered, looking harassed. The last time he'd looked this way a russet haired, cinnamon-eyed American had been the cause.

'I thought you'd finished for the day,' he told his aide.

'Almost, Your Majesty.'

'Did you see Milena?'

'I did. She is fine. The dress-fitting went very well.'

That surprised him. He still didn't know if his sister really want to marry the Prince of Toran. She hadn't said. In fact she hadn't said anything much to him these past few days, still angry with him for banning her from seeing Chad James. But what had she expected? That he would welcome their friendship with open arms? The man was lucky enough to still have a job. A concession he'd only made because of Regan.

'Good. So what's put that look on your face?'

'The PR department are querying the statement about the end of your engagement to Miss James…'

'What of it?'

'Well, sir, they'd like to know when you plan to release it to the media?'

Jag swivelled his chair to stare out at the dusky night sky. It was orange and mauve, almost a replica of the night he'd lain with Regan by the side of the lagoon. 'When I'm ready. I'm still not happy with the wording.'

'The wording, sir?'

'I don't want there to be any fallout for Miss James. I want the responsibility for what has happened to fall on my shoulders, not hers.'

'Admirable, Your Majesty, but it's a bit late for that.'

Jag's eyes narrowed as he studied his trusted aide. 'What are you talking about?' he asked, as fingers of unease whispered across the nape of his neck.

'The Press have been hounding Miss James ever since she returned to America, sir. I thought that, with the release of the statement ending your engagement, that might ease up for her.'

'What do you mean, the Press have been hounding her? I organised a full security detail to accompany Regan on the jet home. They were to keep the Press at bay for as long as necessary once she got there.'

'Miss James took a commercial flight home, sir.'

Jag surged to his feet, every muscle in his body tight. 'Why wasn't I told about this?' he asked with a deadly sense of calm.

'Because the staff are too afraid to mention her name around you, Your Majesty.'

'You're not.'

'Actually I...' His aide flushed. 'After I returned the ring to you I dared not saying anything again. But if you don't mind me asking, sir, why did you let her go? I thought she was wonderful for you. All the staff did.'

Why had he let her go?

Because he hadn't had any choice. He'd wronged her. A woman whose company he enjoyed. A woman he had come to respect above all others. A woman he had... A rush of emotion threatened to overtake him and he ruthlessly drove it back. This time, though, his formidable mind failed him. This time the emotions kept surging.

'The heart knows what the heart wants.'

Was it possible? Had he fallen in love with

Regan? Logic told him that he hadn't spent enough time with her for that to happen but his heart wasn't listening.

He stared at his aide as all the pieces finally fell into place. 'Fear,' he enunciated succinctly, reefing his jacket from the hanger near his door and striding out of his office. 'Nothing but fear.'

'Are they still outside?'

'Still outside?' Penny turned from glancing out of the sitting-room window of Regan's apartment. 'They're outside, up the street, and in the trees. In fact I think there are more of them today than yesterday.'

Regan sighed. 'I was hoping they'd have started to lose interest by now.'

'This is ridiculous, Regan,' Penny snapped. 'You have to do something about it. They've been chasing after you like you're an animal. It's terrible.'

'I know. But what can I do? I told them I wasn't with the King any more but they don't believe me.'

Penny pulled a face. 'Once you become mistress to the King—voila, instant celebrity as far as the Press is concerned.'

'Who would want it?' Regan groaned into her hands. 'And I wasn't his mistress.'

'You did say you slept with him.'

'One night. That hardly makes me his mistress.'

'You know you blush every time you mention him, don't you? Was the sex that good?'

Regan blushed harder.

'Don't answer that.' Penny sighed. 'One day I want great sex like that. Even if it is just for one night.'

'You don't,' Regan returned. 'Believe me, I've been practising getting over him and…' Her voice choked up. 'I'm getting there.'

Regan knew from losing her parents that time healed all wounds. And when it didn't it at least dulled the pain to a manageable level. Unfortunately that didn't seem to be happening yet.

'I suppose in hindsight agreeing to pose as his fiancée was really naive,' Regan admitted. 'I thought there would be less fallout from that but there's been more.'

'That's because it's a romance story for the ages. Everyone wants it to be true.' She took a long sip of coffee. 'Whatever happened to the press release you said you signed?'

'I don't know.' Regan frowned; the lack of a press release had continued to perturb her. 'He must have only put it out locally.'

'It wouldn't matter if he'd put it out in the palace toilets...the world would still know about it by now.'

Regan gave Penny a faint smile. Having her by her side the past week had been a godsend. Penny had taken one look at her face the first day back at work and shuffled her into the staffroom and closed the door behind them, giving her a hug. Having been through heartache herself, she understood the signs.

The other teachers at the school hadn't been so understanding, some asking her intimate questions about what the King was like, obviously looking for some insider's scoop, and others upset because she had brought a cavalcade of media to the school gates and it just wasn't done.

'Have you had another look online?' Penny asked.

Regan didn't want to look online. When she did she was bombarded with photo after photo of herself and the King. It was too painful to look at.

'At least if you called the palace you could ask

about it,' Penny persisted. 'Regan, you have a right to live your life without being harassed.' She slapped her mug on the counter. 'Give me the number. If you're not going to call, I will. It's not as if they'll put me through to the King or anything.'

'Penny, I love you for wanting to help but I don't think it will. I—'

A hard rap at the door brought both their heads around. 'How did they get up here? You have a security door downstairs.'

'Maybe one of the neighbours accidentally let them through,' Regan whispered.

Penny went to the window again and peered outside. 'Well, don't answer the door whatever you do—I can't see a single photographer outside, which means that they're all piled up against your front door.'

Regan groaned. 'What am I going to do?'

'Regan! I know you're in there. Open the door.'

Regan froze, her eyes flying to Penny's.

'Damn, but whoever that is they have a yummy voice,' Penny said. 'Pity they're probably scum as well.'

'It's him.'

Penny frowned. 'Who?'

Regan had to swallow before she could get the words out. 'The King,' she whispered.

'Are you sure?'

'Regan!'

Regan nodded. 'I'd know his voice anywhere.'

'Good lord…what do you think he wants?'

'I have no idea.'

'Regan, please open the door.'

Penny raised a brow. 'He said please that time. Do you want me to get it?'

Regan shook her head. 'I will.'

On legs that felt like overcooked spaghetti, Regan walked to the door and opened it. As soon as she did her heart stopped beating. When it started again it jumped into her mouth.

Jag stood on her doorstep with what looked like two paratroopers behind him, a dark scowl on his face. 'You're lucky you answered it when you did. I was just about to break it down.'

'Why?'

'I thought something had happened to you. You haven't answered a single call I've made in the last ten hours.'

'Oh.' Still trying to take in the fact that he was here, in New York, on her doorstep, she stared at him blankly. 'I've stopped carrying my phone around with me because it never stops ringing.'

'Do you know how dangerous that is?'

'At the minute I go from work to home and back again. Anything else is impossible.'

'That's because you didn't take the security detail I organised for you. That was not a good call.'

'You're not responsible for me.'

'The hell I'm not.' His blue eyes turned fierce. 'Didn't you think something like this would happen? That the paparazzi would want your story?'

'No. I told you my world is usually a lot smaller than yours. I didn't know what to expect until I got here and then...'

'You should have called me to tell me!'

'I wasn't sure you'd take my call.' And she couldn't have lived with that. 'Listen, I'm fine. I appreciate your concern but... I can cope.'

He ran his eyes over her and she felt terribly exposed in her cut-off shorts and worn T-shirt.

'I know you can cope. You're the strongest woman I've ever met.' He dragged a hand through his hair and her pulse rocketed at the memory of how it had felt on her fingers.

The air between them seemed to throb as it

usually did when he was this close, and she saw him swallow heavily.

'We're not having this conversation out here, Regan.' He strode past her into her flat and Regan felt helpless to stop him.

She nearly ran smack into the back of him when he stopped in the doorway to her living room.

'Who are you?'

'I'm ah… I'm ah… Penny, Regan's friend.'

'Well, Penny, Regan's friend, I'm King Jaeger of Santara, Regan's fiancée, and I'd really like to talk to her alone.'

'Oh, sure. Of course.' Penny seemed to visibly pull herself together at being confronted by royalty. 'Well, that is, if it's okay with Regan.'

Regan was still trying to process what he had just announced. 'You're not still my fiancée.'

He turned his piercing blue eyes on her. 'Actually I am. I haven't officially ended things between us yet.'

'You haven't…' She frowned. 'I gave you back the ring and Milena is home. The deal ended then.'

'I'm changing the terms of it.'

'You can't do that.'

He looked at her with patient exasperation. 'Will you please give your friend permission to leave? Unless you want an audience for the rest of this conversation.'

'Oh, sorry. Yes, Penny, I'm fine. He won't hurt me.'

At least he wouldn't intentionally hurt her, but looking at him, being this close to him… Her chest felt tight with the strain of holding her emotions inside.

'I'll call you,' Penny promised before slipping out of the door. When it clicked closed behind her Regan had to place her hand over her chest to keep her emotions back. It was only then that she noticed how dishevelled and tired he looked.

'Look, I know you feel responsible about the paparazzi,' she began, 'but I don't know how you can fix it. I don't want to walk around town swamped by security guards. It will only make things worse. Did you release the press statement yet? Penny thinks that will make it easier.' She pulled a face. 'Even without the ring, they refuse to believe we're not still together. They think I'm trying to play coy.'

She plonked herself down on her favourite armchair and remembered the shelling of questions she'd received ever since landing back in New York.

'*Where's the King? When is he planning to visit you?*'

'*Have you set a wedding date yet?*'

'*Give us a smile, Regan. Tell us how you met.*'

She'd even been invited on a talk show.

'I didn't release the statement,' he said, pacing around her small flat and dwarfing it with his superior size.

'Why not? And what do you mean, you're changing the terms of our deal? Why would you want to do that?'

'Because I was wrong, and that's not easy for me to admit.' He came to stand in front of her. 'You were right when you said that Milena didn't want to marry the Prince of Toran. She doesn't. At least, she doesn't yet. You'll be happy to know that I spoke to her on my way over here and the wedding has been postponed for a year. I've also agreed that she can resume her job at GeoTech and keep working with your brother.'

'That's really nice of you. But you know you're not responsible for Milena's actions, don't you?'

'Not completely no, but after her health scare a few years back I stopped listening to what she wanted and thought I knew best. A mistake I don't want to make with you.'

'How could you make that mistake with me?'

'By presuming you want the same thing that I do.' He squatted down in front of her so they were at eye level.

Regan's heart leapt into her throat. 'What is it you want?'

'You.'

'Me?'

He gave her a small smile. 'When you left, *habiba*, you took a part of me with you. A part of me I wasn't even aware existed.'

The bleak look in his eyes made her feel suddenly hot and cold all over. 'What did I take?'

'My heart, *habiba*; you took my heart.'

A bubble of something that felt faintly like hope swelled inside her chest. 'What are you saying?'

He released a heavy sigh, his eyes full of emotion when they met hers. 'I'm saying that I love you.'

'But that's impossible.'

'You doubt it?' He gave a self-deprecating laugh. 'I detained you. I bound you to my side by making you my fiancée.'

'For your sister.'

'I told myself that too, but the truth is you got under my skin from the first moment I saw you in that shisha bar, and every decision I made from then on defied logic and reason. That should have been my first clue.'

Regan felt dazed. Dizzy. 'But you don't believe in love.'

'That's not strictly true, *ya amar.*' He gave her a small smile. 'I do believe in it. I just didn't think I needed it.' He took her trembling hands and drew her to her feet. 'The thing is, Regan, I'm hopeless when it comes to emotions. All my life it's been easier to shut down than to expose myself to pain. If you don't feel anything you don't hurt.' He gave a sharp laugh as if the concept was ludicrous to him now. 'It was that simple. I thought it made me stronger. I convinced myself a long time ago that I didn't need love in my life—I even thought I wasn't able to feel it— but I was wrong. I just didn't realise *how* wrong until I lost you.'

'You didn't lose me,' Regan said softly, stepping closer to him. 'I only left because I thought you didn't want me.'

He shook his head. 'Not want you? I can't stop wanting you.'

'Then why did you always find it so easy to turn away from me?'

'Practice. But I'm sick of practising walking away. It's what both my parents did my whole life and I didn't even know I'd taken on that part of them until you left. Now I want to practise staying put. I want to practise being open. I want to practise being in love. With you.'

Regan smiled so wide her cheeks hurt. 'You do?'

'I do.' A slow smile started on his face. 'Will you have me, *habiba*, flaws and all?'

'Only if you'll have me, flaws and all.'

'You have none.'

Regan laughed. 'Now I know you really do love me because I have loads.'

He swung her into his arms, his head coming down to hers for a desperate, heated kiss. 'I've missed you, *habiba*. Tell me you've missed me too.'

'Oh, Jag, I have.' Happiness swelled inside her chest. 'I really have.'

'Regan, *ya amar*...' He kissed her again. Harder. Deeper. 'I love you, so much.'

Regan stared at him dreamily. 'I can't really believe it.'

'Believe it, *habiba*. Do you remember that photo you took of me with Arrow? The one in the desert?'

'Yes.'

'You asked me what I was thinking when you took it and I told you that I didn't remember.' He smoothed her hair back from her face. 'Ask me again.'

'What were you thinking?' she asked dreamily.

'I was thinking how happy I was being in the desert with you. I was thinking that I couldn't remember ever being that happy before.'

Regan couldn't contain her joy and didn't try. 'I was thinking the exact same thing. You looked so magnificent I couldn't take my eyes off you.'

Jag dragged her mouth back to his, his hands skating over her back, holding her tightly. Finally he lifted his head, groaning with the effort. 'I want forever with you, *habiba*. Can you give me that, even though it means you'll be the centre of everyone's attention for ever and a day?'

'Jag, I could give you anything at all as long as I'm the centre of *your* attention.'

'*Habiba*, you already are. You're the centre of my world.'

EPILOGUE

MILENA STOOD BEHIND Regan and adjusted the train on her ivory wedding dress.

'You look so beautiful,' she murmured, misty-eyed.

Regan smiled, unable to believe that today was her wedding day. 'Thank you. I feel so nervous and I don't know why.'

'Bridal nerves,' Milena said, smoothing down her own rose-gold gown. 'But you don't have to worry about my brother. You've transformed him. I've never seen him so happy and it fills my heart with joy.'

'He makes me happy too. These past three months of being with him have given me more happiness than I could have ever hoped to feel.'

More than she had ever expected to feel. For so many years she had put her own needs aside and, although she would never regret any of those years, being with Jag had made her truly blossom. She gazed at the solid-gold bracelet on her wrist that he had given her as a pre-wedding present. The jeweller had inlaid a photo of her parents on their wedding day and she stroked a finger across their smiling faces. 'Thank you,' she murmured. 'For loving me and in the process showing me how to love in turn.'

Tears formed behind her eyes and she blinked them back. Jag had given it as a token of his love, asking that she be patient with him if he ever forgot how to express his feelings towards her, but she hadn't needed to be. He told her he loved her every time he looked at her, his eyes alight with emotion.

Milena stopped fussing with her veil. 'You already feel like the sister I never had, and I want you to know that I'm well aware that you're the reason my brother is allowing me to go and study in London later in the year.'

'You'll always be his little sister, and he'll always worry about you. But I think you're doing the right thing.'

'I do too. And I can't believe the Crown Prince is still willing to marry me even though I'm postponing things. But I want what you and my brother have and I'm determined not to settle for anything less.'

Regan smiled. 'Good for you. I can promise you that it's worth the wait.'

Brimming with happiness, Regan turned when Penny poked her head around the corner. 'You'd better get out here,' she said, stern-faced. 'Your King isn't going to wait for ever, Reggie. He looks like he's about to come tearing down the aisle and drag you to the altar himself.'

Regan grinned. She wouldn't put it past him and she wouldn't mind a bit. All her life she'd dreamed of finding a love that could rival her parents' and she had. Feeling her nerves finally settle, she took a deep breath. 'Where's Chad?'

'Waiting.'

Regan nodded and stepped onto the red carpet. The assembled crowd gave a collective gasp as they saw her. Chad stepped forward. 'You look beautiful, sis.' His eyes, the same shade of brown as her own, sparkled into hers.

'I love you, you know that, right?' she said softly.

He gave her a tiny smile. 'I love you too. Now, let's move before your possessive fiancé accuses me of holding up the wedding proceedings.'

Regan laughed, and placed her hand in the crook of his arm. 'Then let's go,' she said, turning to lock eyes with the man of her dreams waiting with barely leashed patience for her to join him at the end of the aisle.

* * * * *

LET'S TALK

Romance

For exclusive extracts, competitions and special offers, find us online:

- facebook.com/millsandboon
- @millsandboonuk
- @millsandboon

Or get in touch on 0844 844 1351*

For all the latest titles coming soon, visit millsandboon.co.uk/nextmonth

*Calls cost 7p per minute plus your phone company's price per minute access charge

Want even more
ROMANCE?

Join our bookclub today!

'Mills & Boon books, the perfect way to escape for an hour or so.'

Miss W. Dyer

'Excellent service, promptly delivered and very good subscription choices.'

Miss A. Pearson

'You get fantastic special offers and the chance to get books before they hit the shops'

Mrs V. Hall

Visit millsandbook.co.uk/Bookclub and save on brand new books.

MILLS & BOON